SCARY GRAPHICS

HOME SWEET HAUNTING

STONE ARCH BOOKS
a capstone imprint

Published by Stone Arch Books, an imprint of Capstone.
1710 Roe Crest Drive
North Mankato, Minnesota 56003
capstonepub.com

Library of Congress Cataloging-in-Publication Data
Names: Mauleón, Daniel, 1991– author. | Brown, Alan, illustrator.
Title: Home sweet haunting / Daniel Mauleón; illustrated by Alan Brown.
Other titles: Scary graphics.
Description: North Mankato, Minnesota : Stone Arch Books, an imprint
of Capstone, [2022] | Series: Scary graphics | Audience: Ages 8–11. |
Audience: Grades 4–6. | Summary: Dominic's family is house hunting,
but as Dominic explores the large Victorian house they are considering,
he encounters a ghost child; when his parents refuse to believe him
Dominic decides to get video evidence—but will he get proof of the
paranormal activity before it is too late?
Identifiers: LCCN 2021006167 (print) | LCCN 2021006168 (ebook)
| ISBN 9781663911643 (hardcover) | ISBN 9781663911650 (pdf) |
ISBN 9781663911674 (kindle edition) Subjects: LCSH: Ghost stories.
| Haunted houses—Juvenile fiction. | Graphic novels. | Horror tales. |
CYAC: Graphic novels. | Ghosts—Fiction. | Haunted houses—Fiction. |
Horror stories. | LCGFT: Graphic novels. | Ghost stories. | Horror fiction.
Classification: LCC PZ7.7.M3884 Hp 2021 (print) | LCC PZ7.7.M3884
(ebook) | DDC 741.5/973—dc23
LC record available at https://lccn.loc.gov/2021006167
LC ebook record available at https://lccn.loc.gov/2021006168

Editor: Julie Gassman
Designers: Tracy Davies and Heidi Thompson
Production Specialist: Tori Abraham

Printed and bound in the USA. 004270

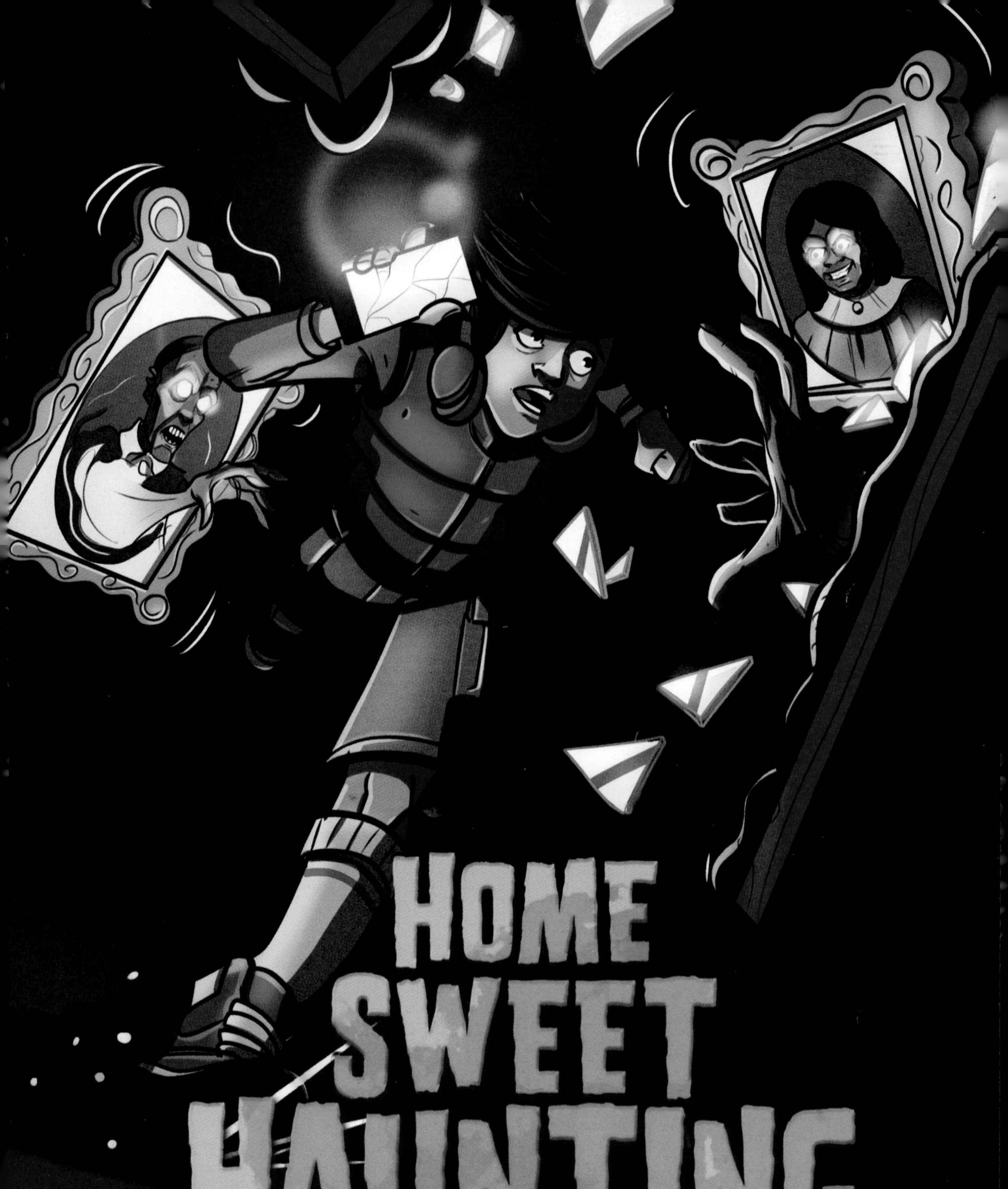

HOME SWEET HAUNTING

BY **DANIEL MAULEÓN**

ILLUSTRATED BY **ALAN BROWN**

WORD OF WARNING:

WHEN HOUSE HUNTING, LOOK CAREFULLY.
YOU NEVER KNOW WHAT MIGHT BE HIDING INSIDE.

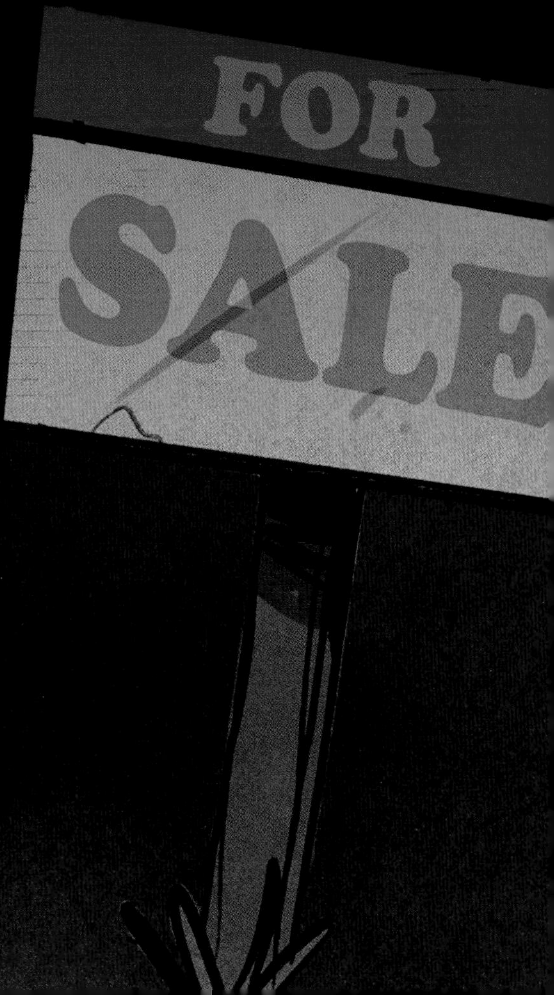
FOR
SALE

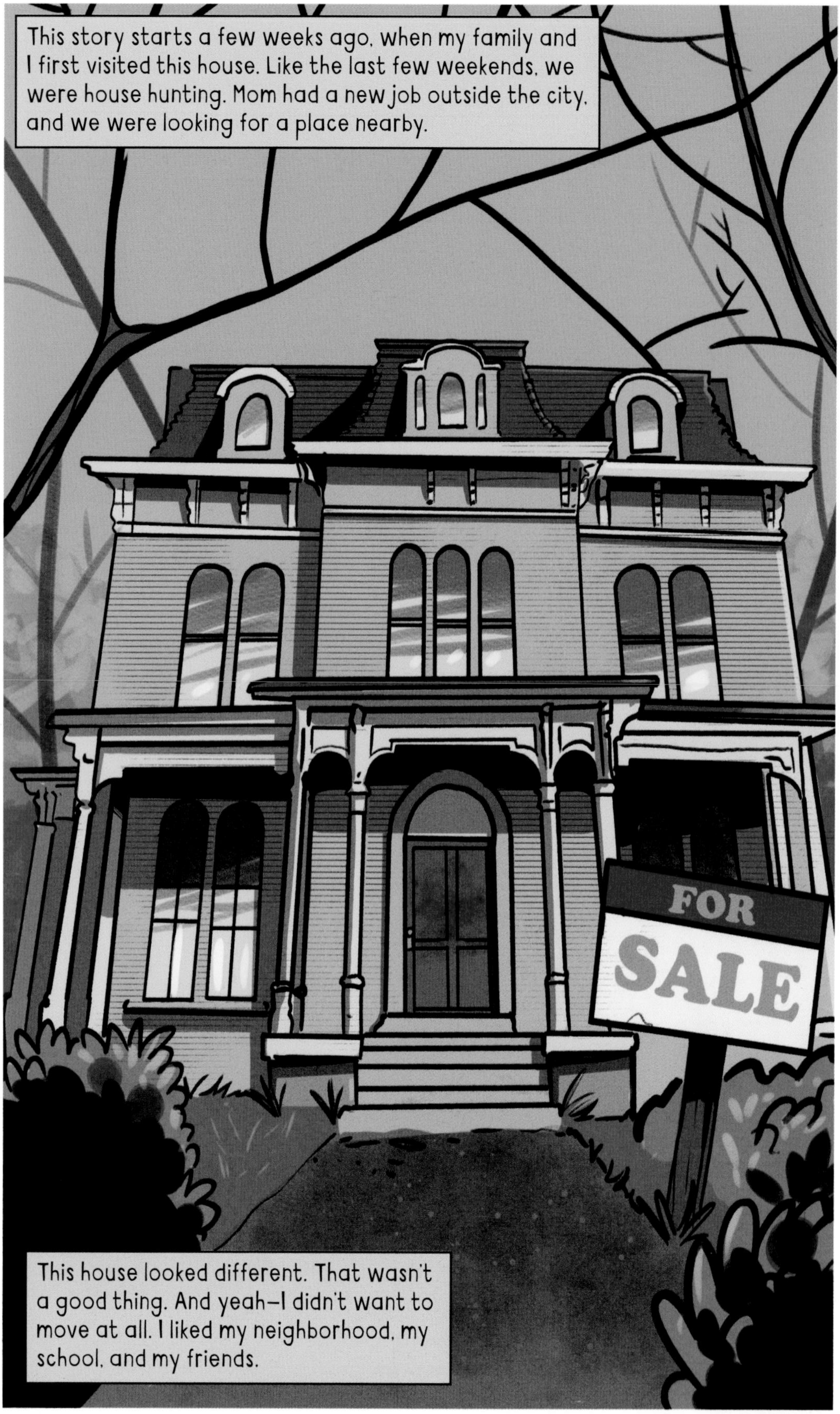
This story starts a few weeks ago, when my family and I first visited this house. Like the last few weekends, we were house hunting. Mom had a new job outside the city, and we were looking for a place nearby.
FOR SALE
This house looked different. That wasn't a good thing. And yeah—I didn't want to move at all. I liked my neighborhood, my school, and my friends.

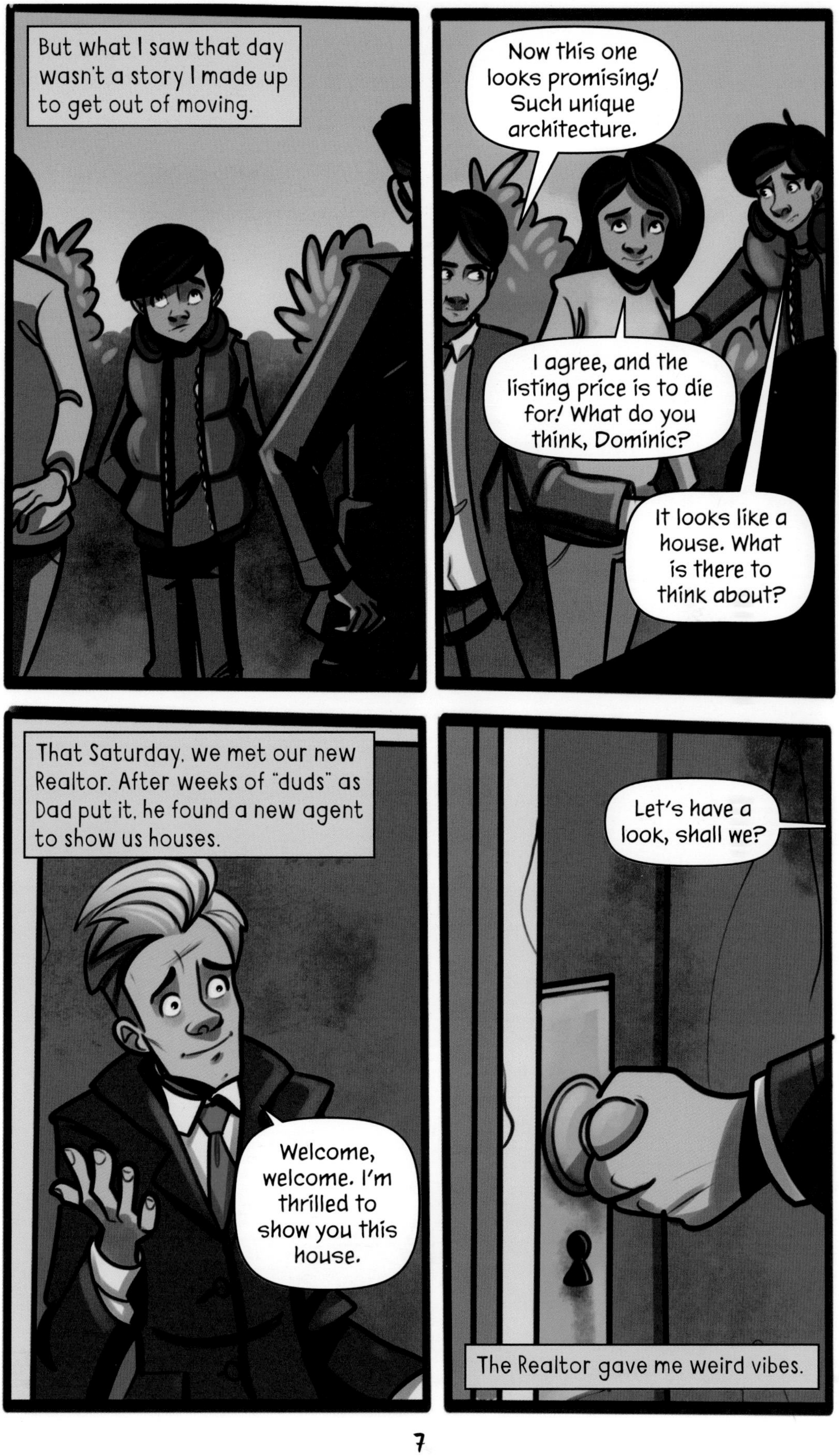
But what I saw that day wasn't a story I made up to get out of moving.
Now this one looks promising! Such unique architecture.
I agree, and the listing price is to die for! What do you think, Dominic?
It looks like a house. What is there to think about?
That Saturday, we met our new Realtor. After weeks of "duds" as Dad put it, he found a new agent to show us houses.
Welcome, welcome. I'm thrilled to show you this house.
Let's have a look, shall we?
The Realtor gave me weird vibes.

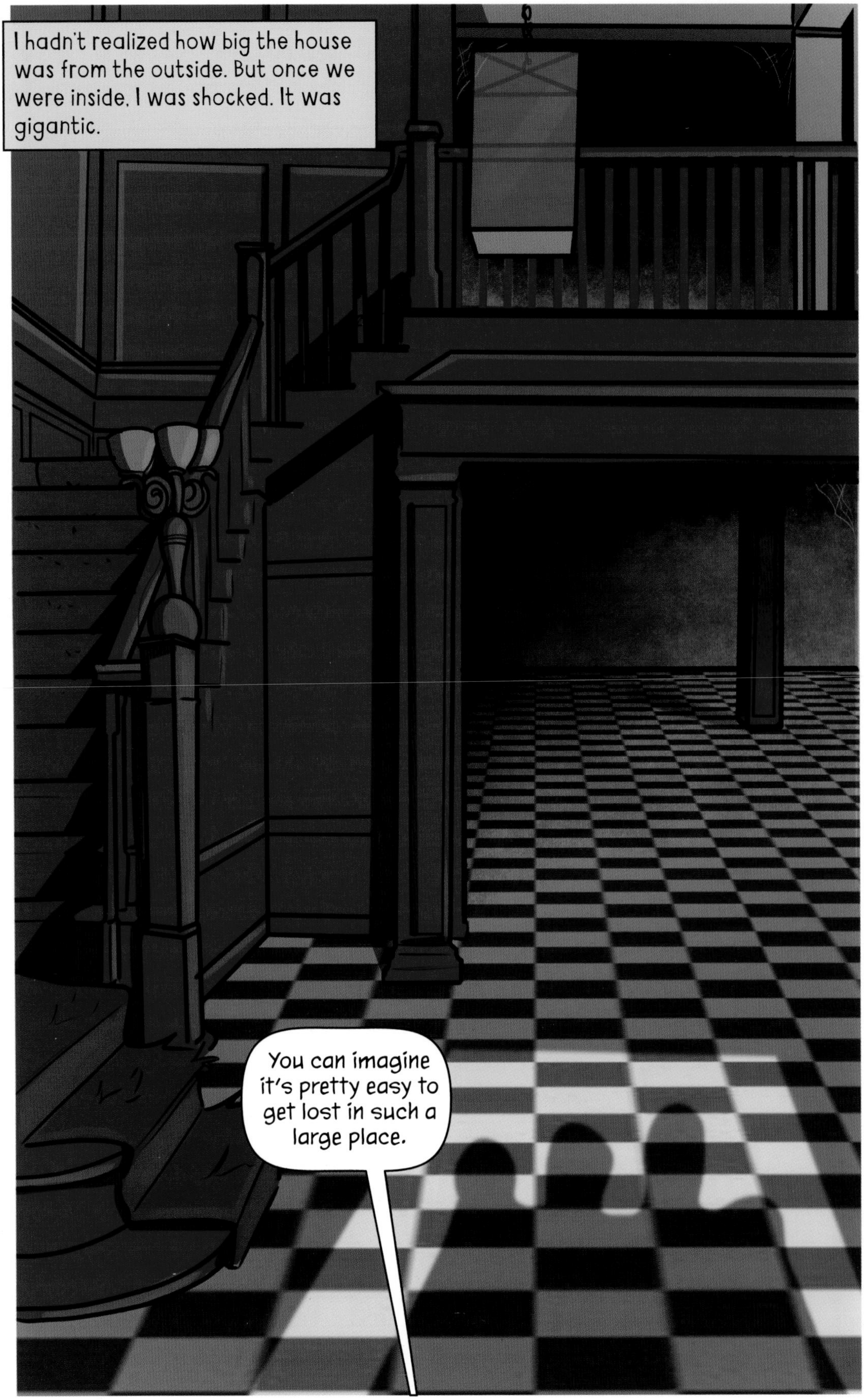
I hadn't realized how big the house was from the outside. But once we were inside, I was shocked. It was gigantic.
You can imagine it's pretty easy to get lost in such a large place.

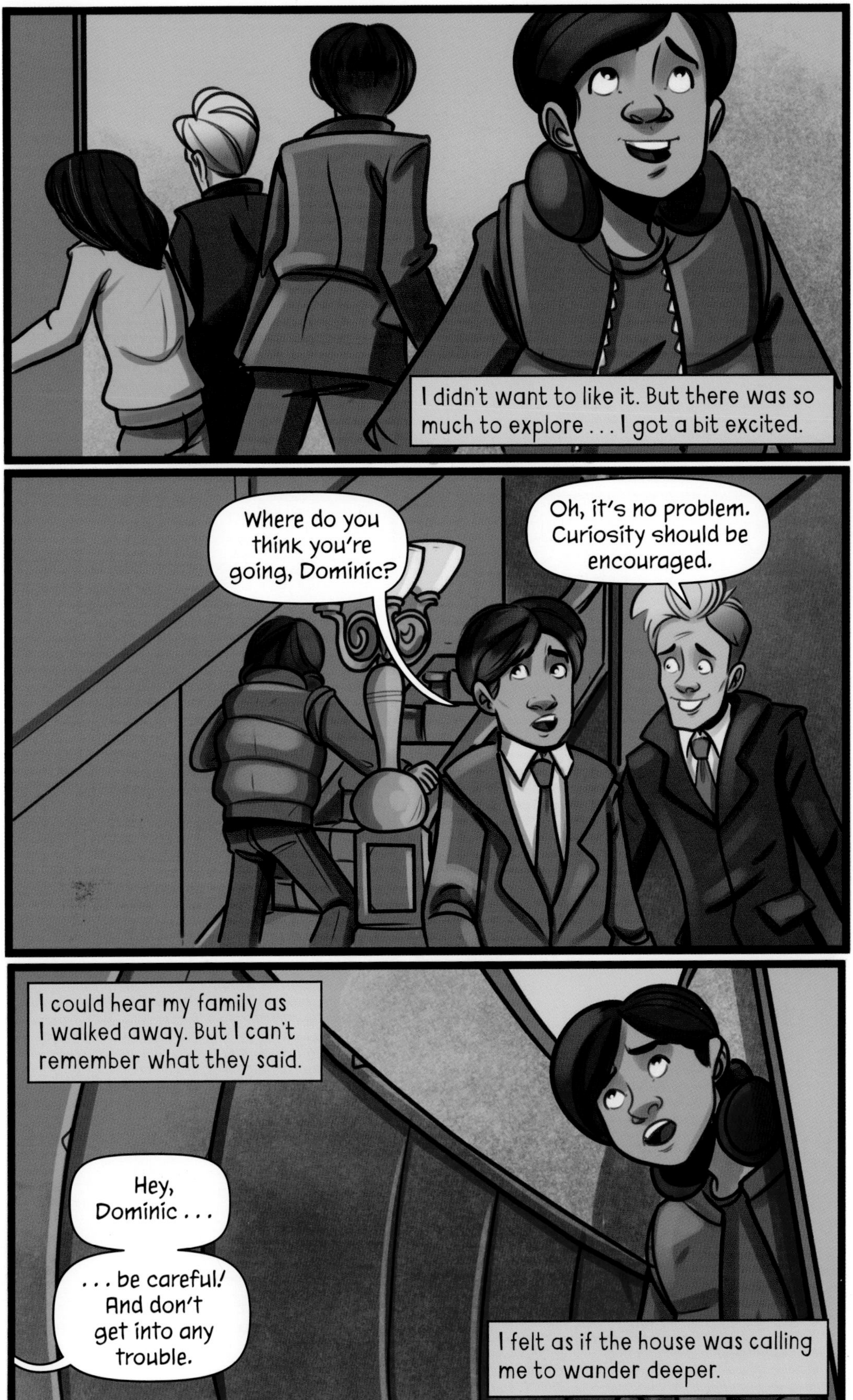
I didn't want to like it. But there was so much to explore . . . I got a bit excited.
Where do you think you're going, Dominic?
Oh, it's no problem. Curiosity should be encouraged.
I could hear my family as I walked away. But I can't remember what they said.
Hey, Dominic . . .
. . . be careful! And don't get into any trouble.
I felt as if the house was calling me to wander deeper.

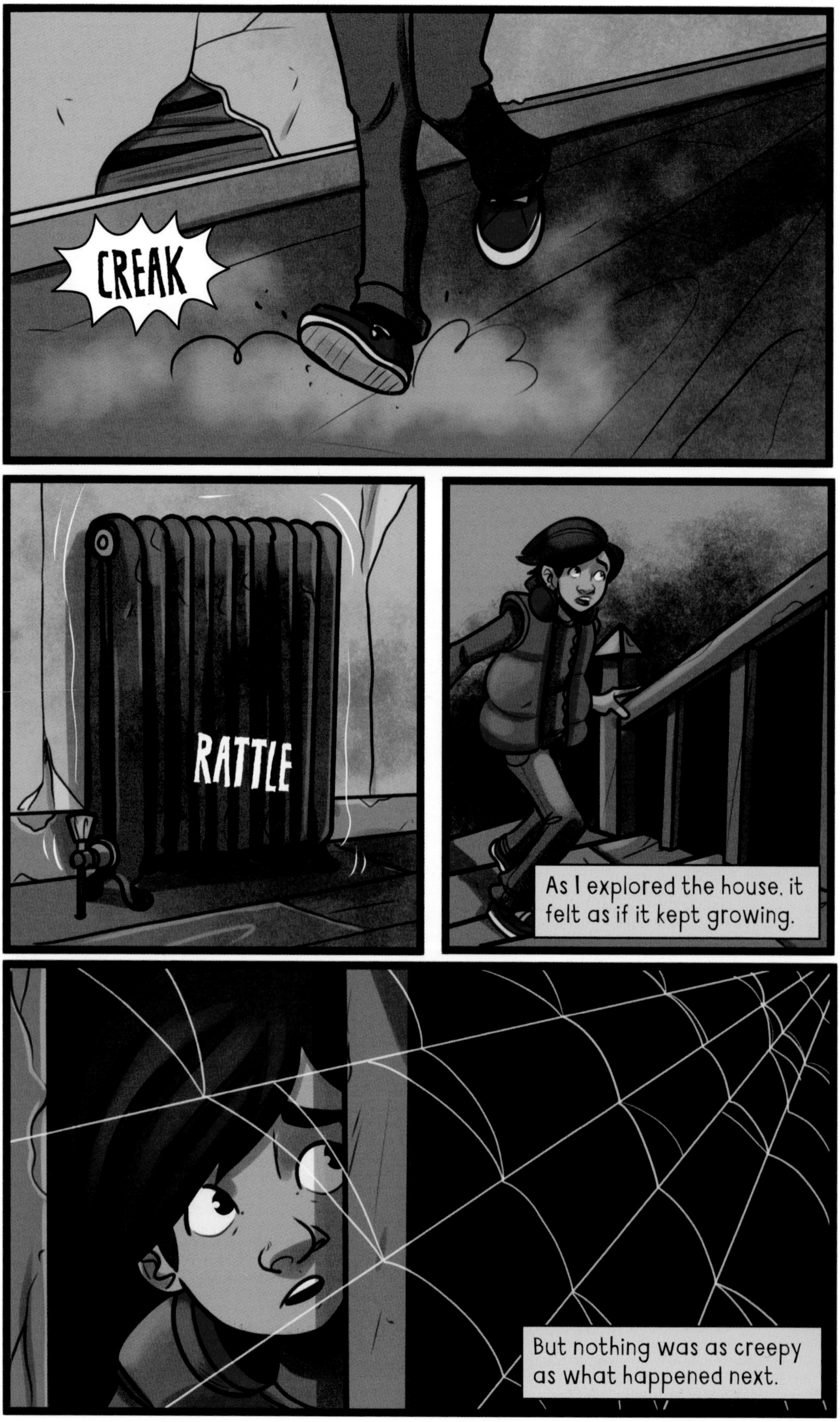
CREAK
RATTLE
As I explored the house, it felt as if it kept growing.
But nothing was as creepy as what happened next.

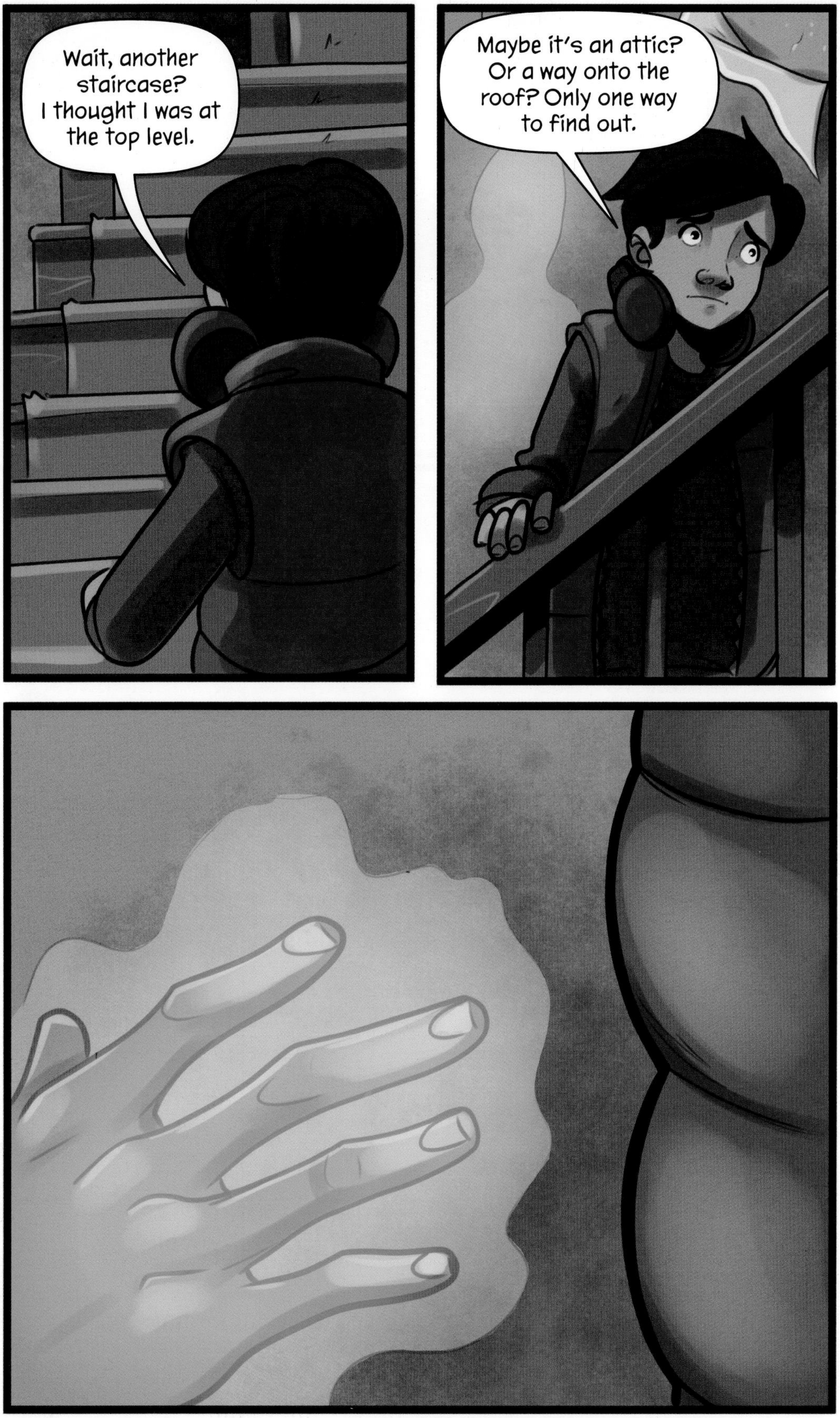
Wait, another staircase? I thought I was at the top level.
Maybe it's an attic? Or a way onto the roof? Only one way to find out.

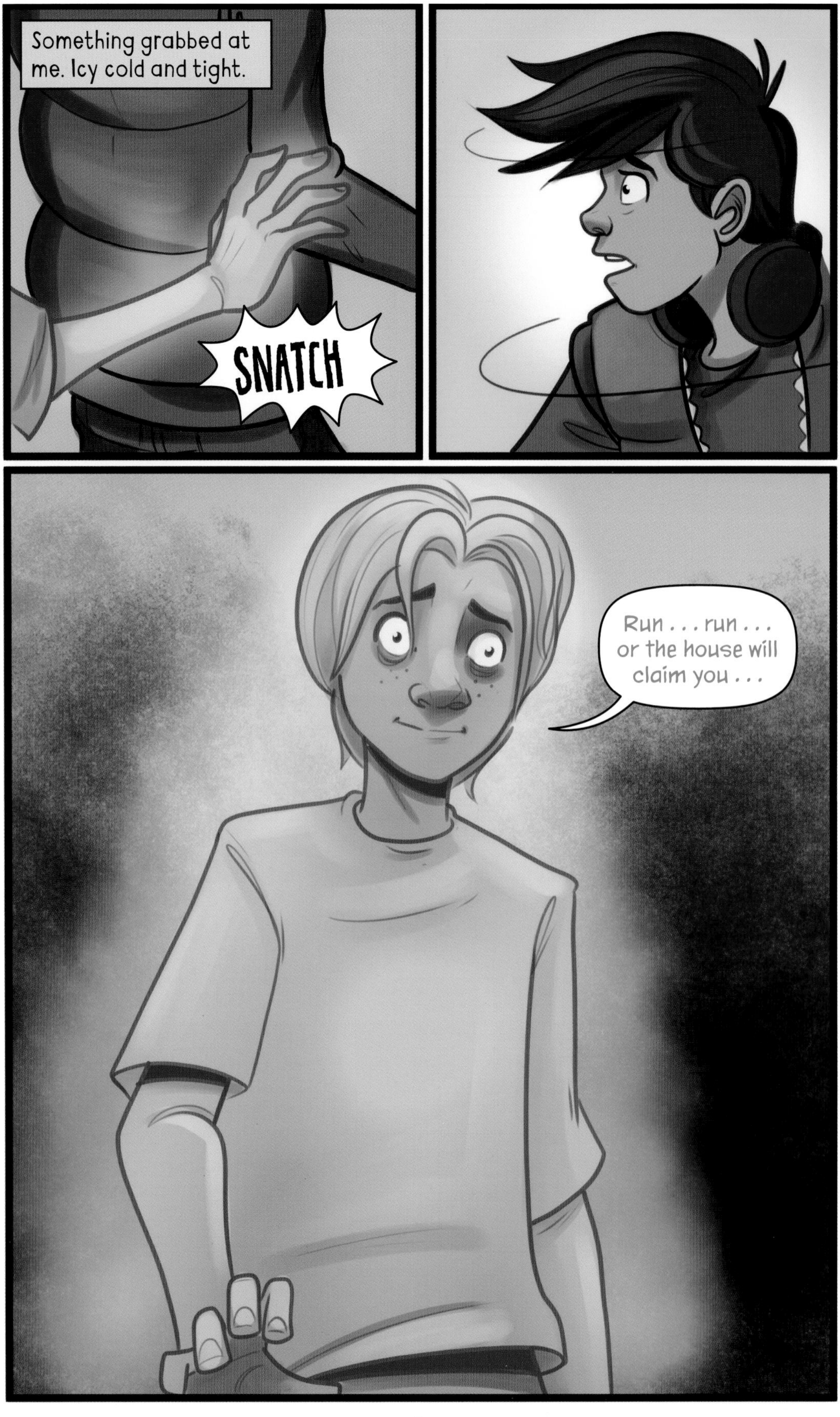
Something grabbed at me. Icy cold and tight.
SNATCH
Run . . . run . . . or the house will claim you . . .

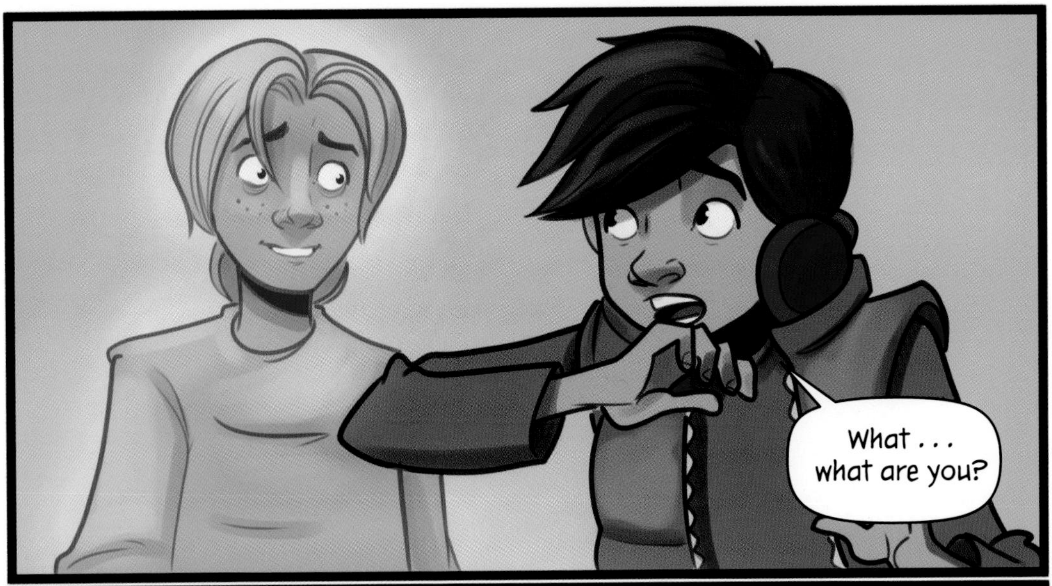
What . . .
what are you?

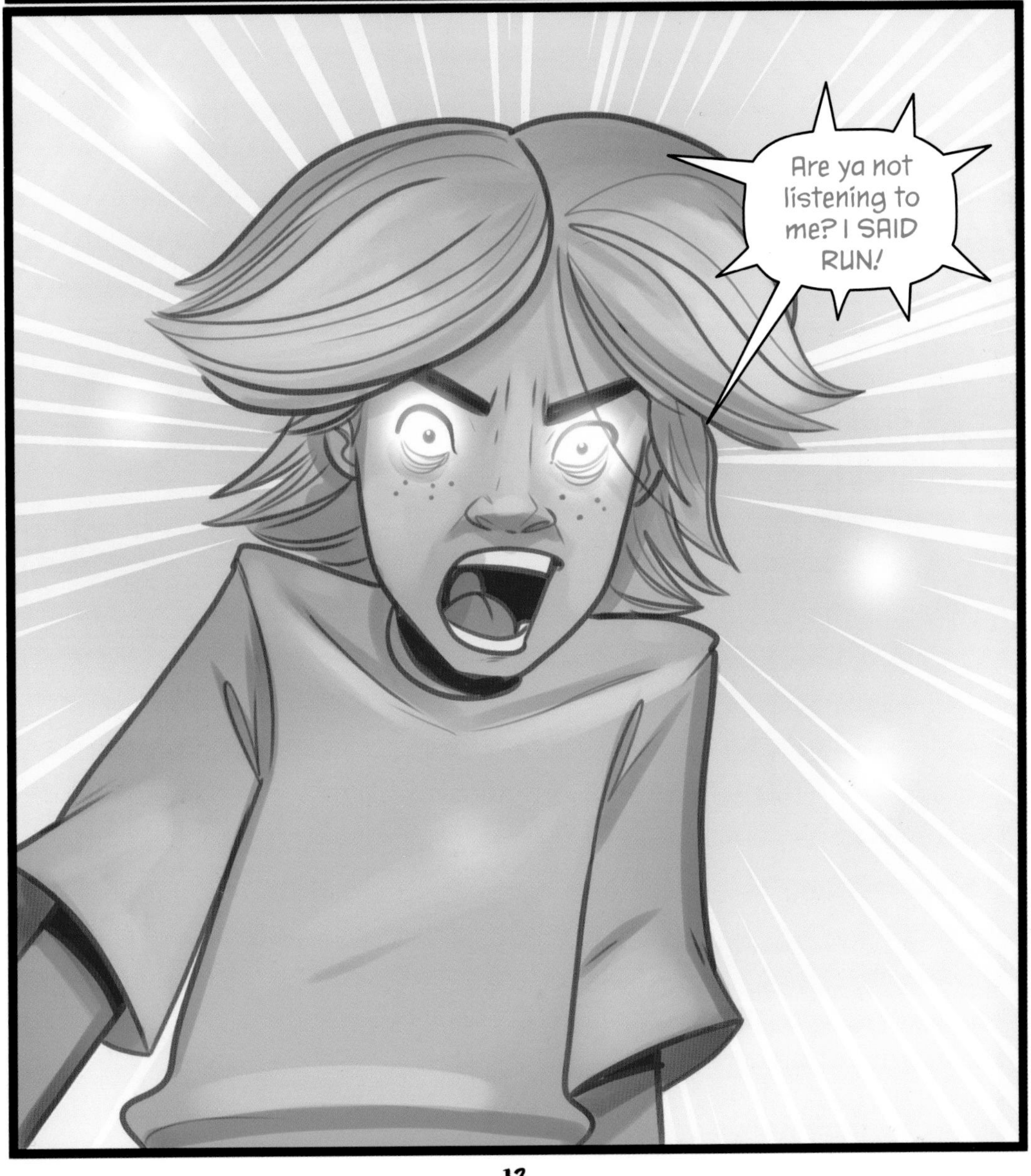
Are ya not listening to me? I SAID RUN!

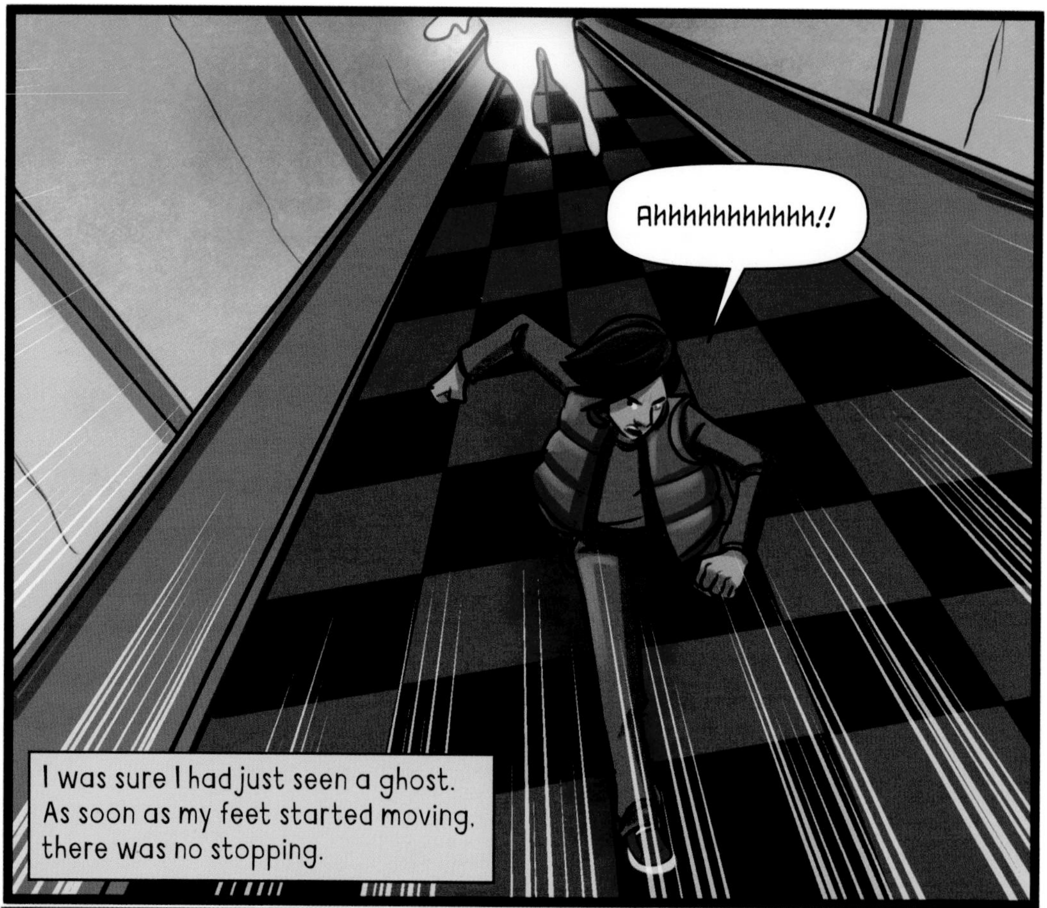
Ahhhhhhhhhhh!!
I was sure I had just seen a ghost. As soon as my feet started moving, there was no stopping.

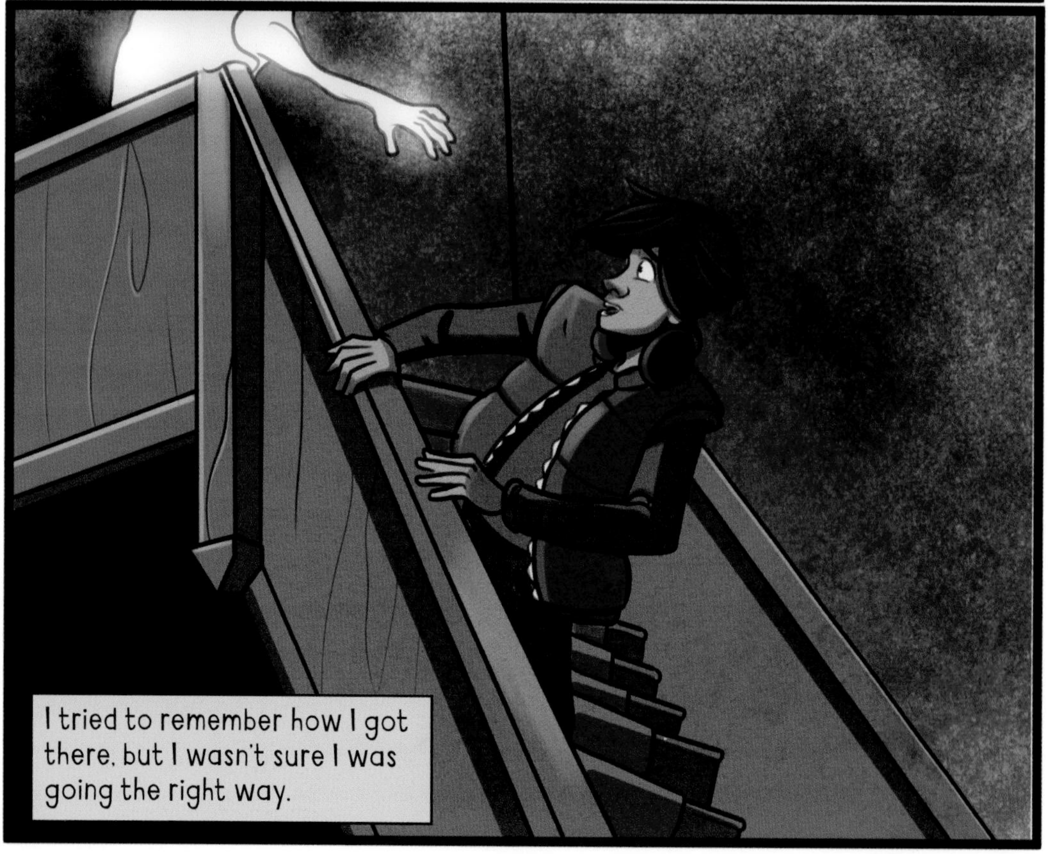
I tried to remember how I got there, but I wasn't sure I was going the right way.

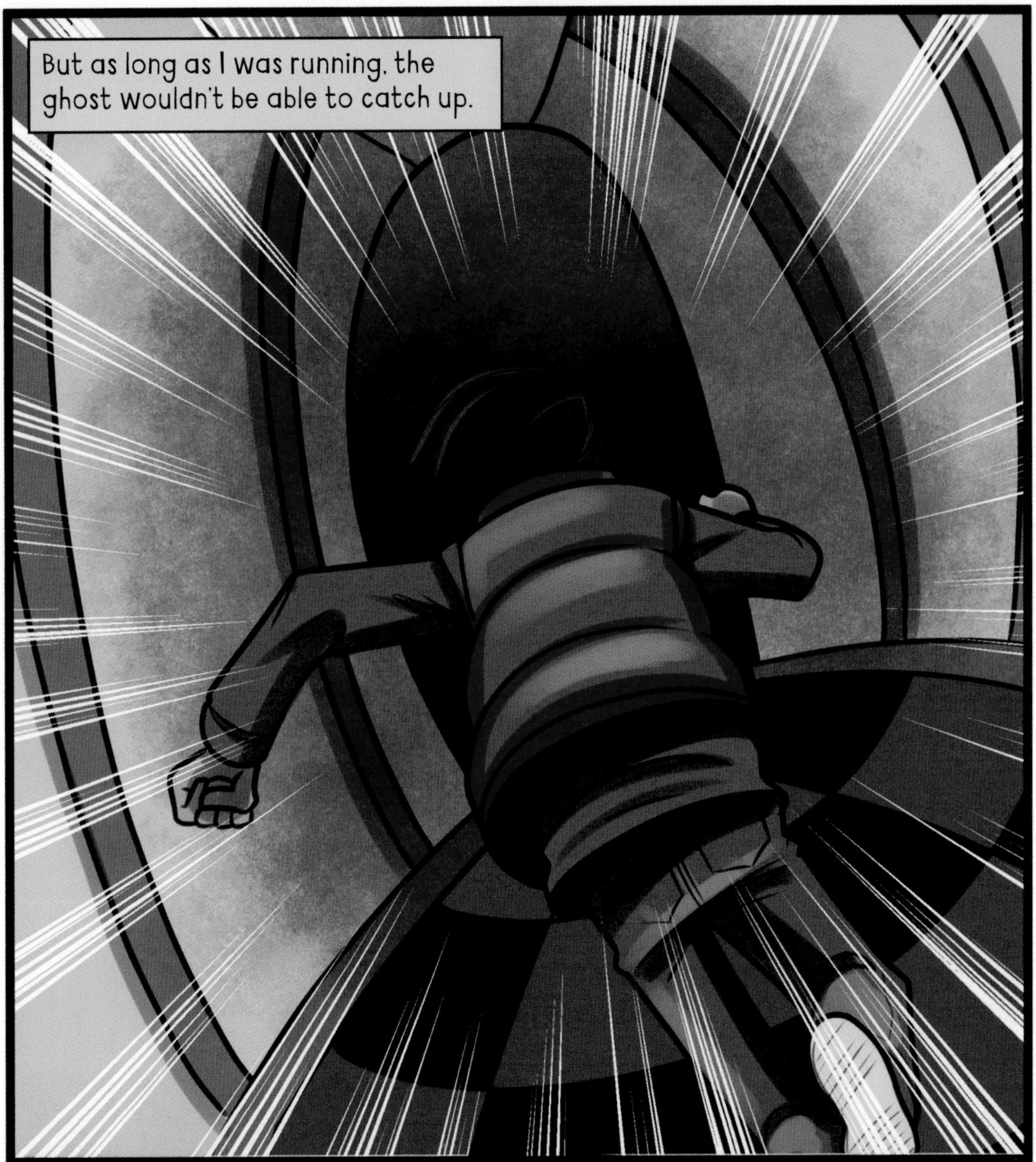
But as long as I was running, the ghost wouldn't be able to catch up.

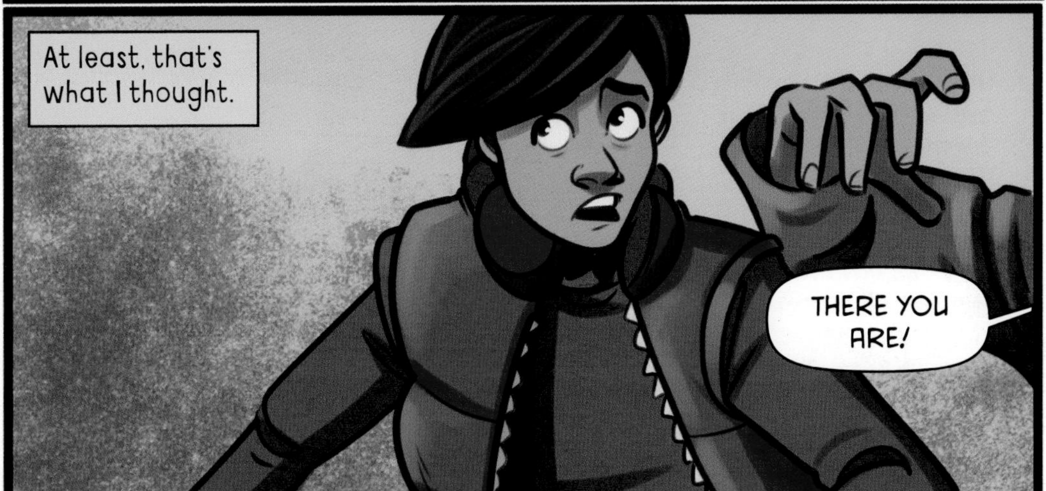
At least, that's what I thought.
THERE YOU ARE!

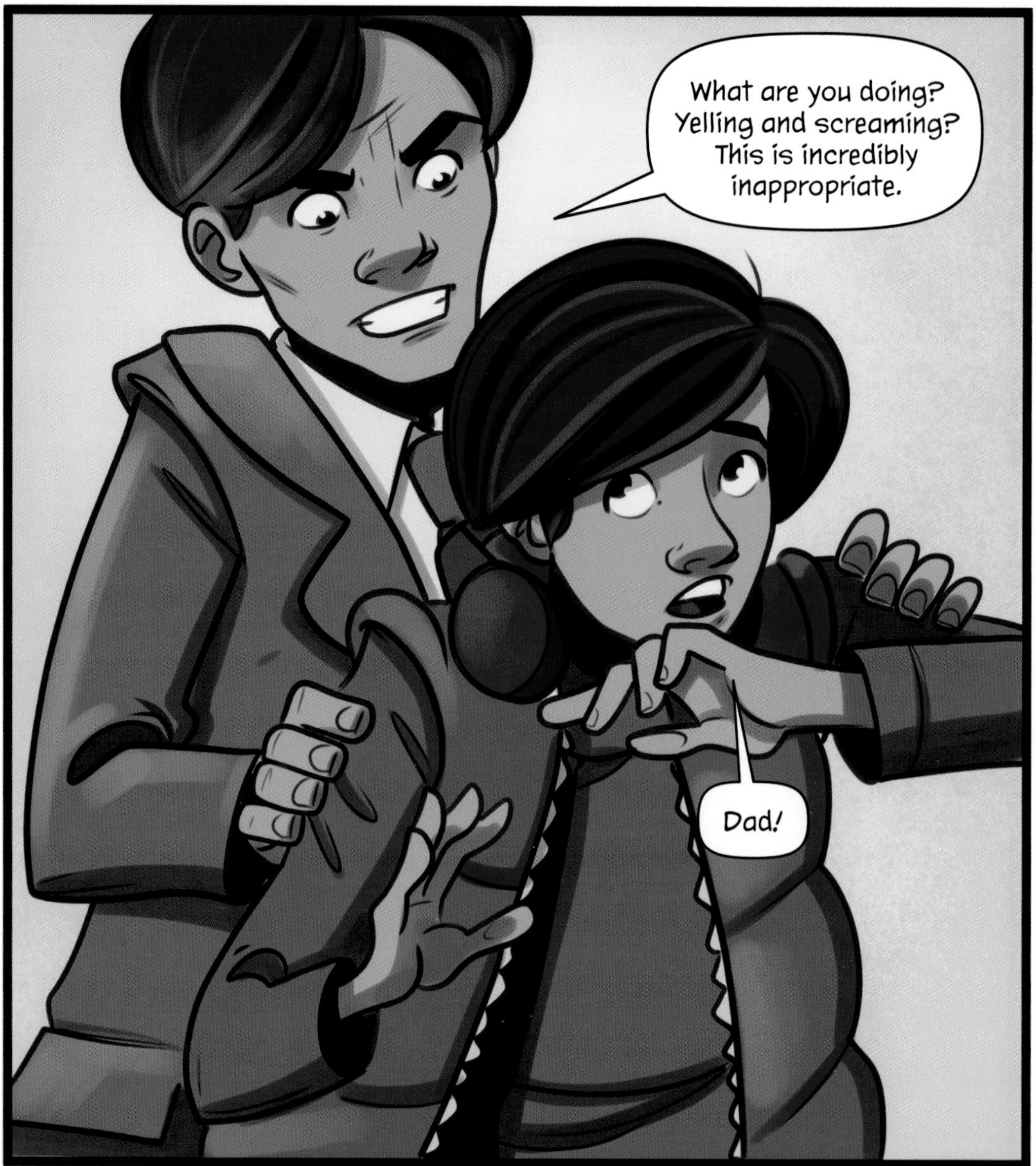
What are you doing? Yelling and screaming? This is incredibly inappropriate.
Dad!

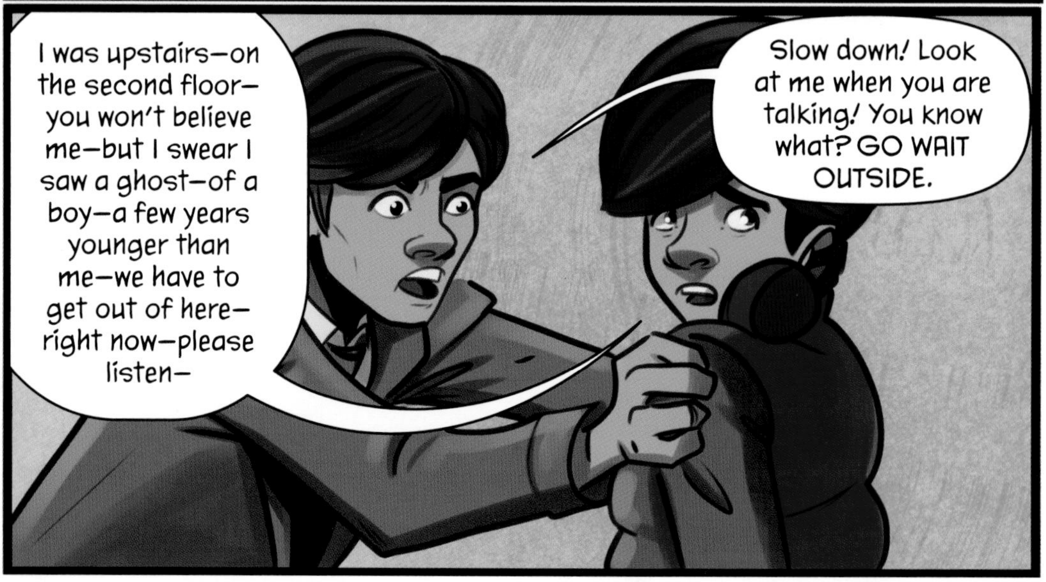
I was upstairs—on the second floor—you won't believe me—but I swear I saw a ghost—of a boy—a few years younger than me—we have to get out of here—right now—please listen—
Slow down! Look at me when you are talking! You know what? GO WAIT OUTSIDE.

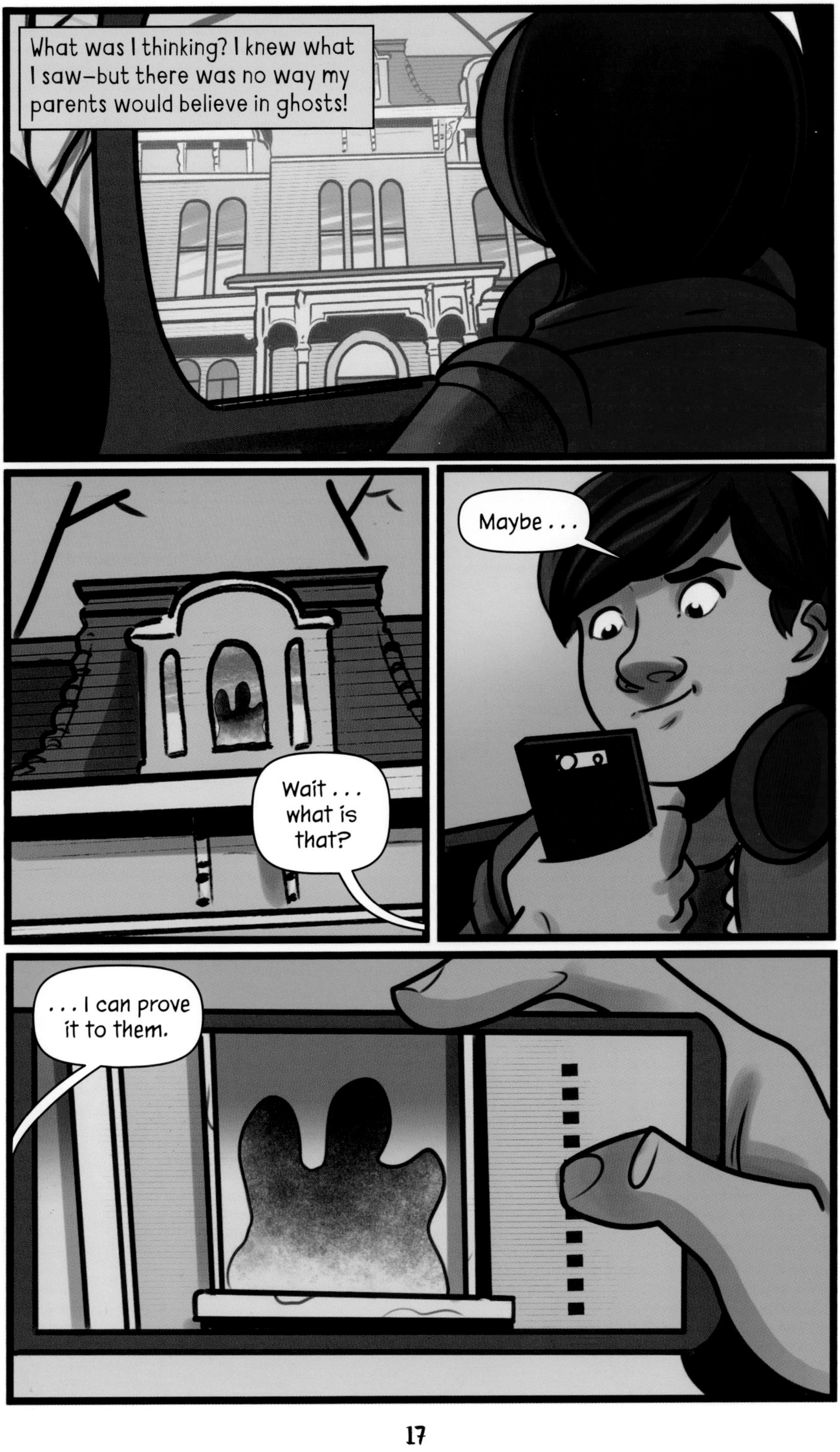
What was I thinking? I knew what I saw—but there was no way my parents would believe in ghosts!
Wait . . . what is that?
Maybe . . .
. . . I can prove it to them.

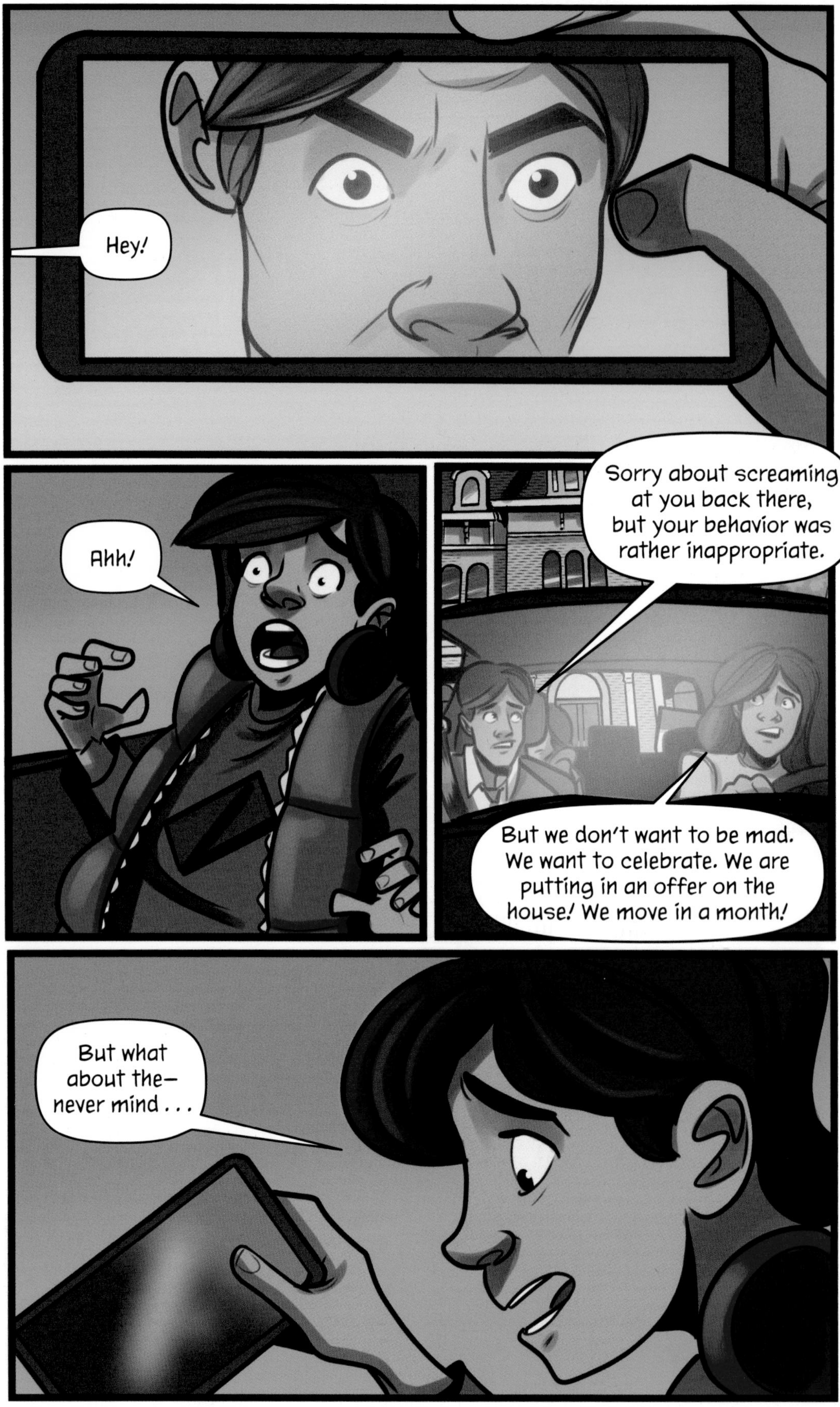
Hey!
Ahh!
Sorry about screaming at you back there, but your behavior was rather inappropriate.
But we don't want to be mad. We want to celebrate. We are putting in an offer on the house! We move in a month!
But what about the— never mind . . .

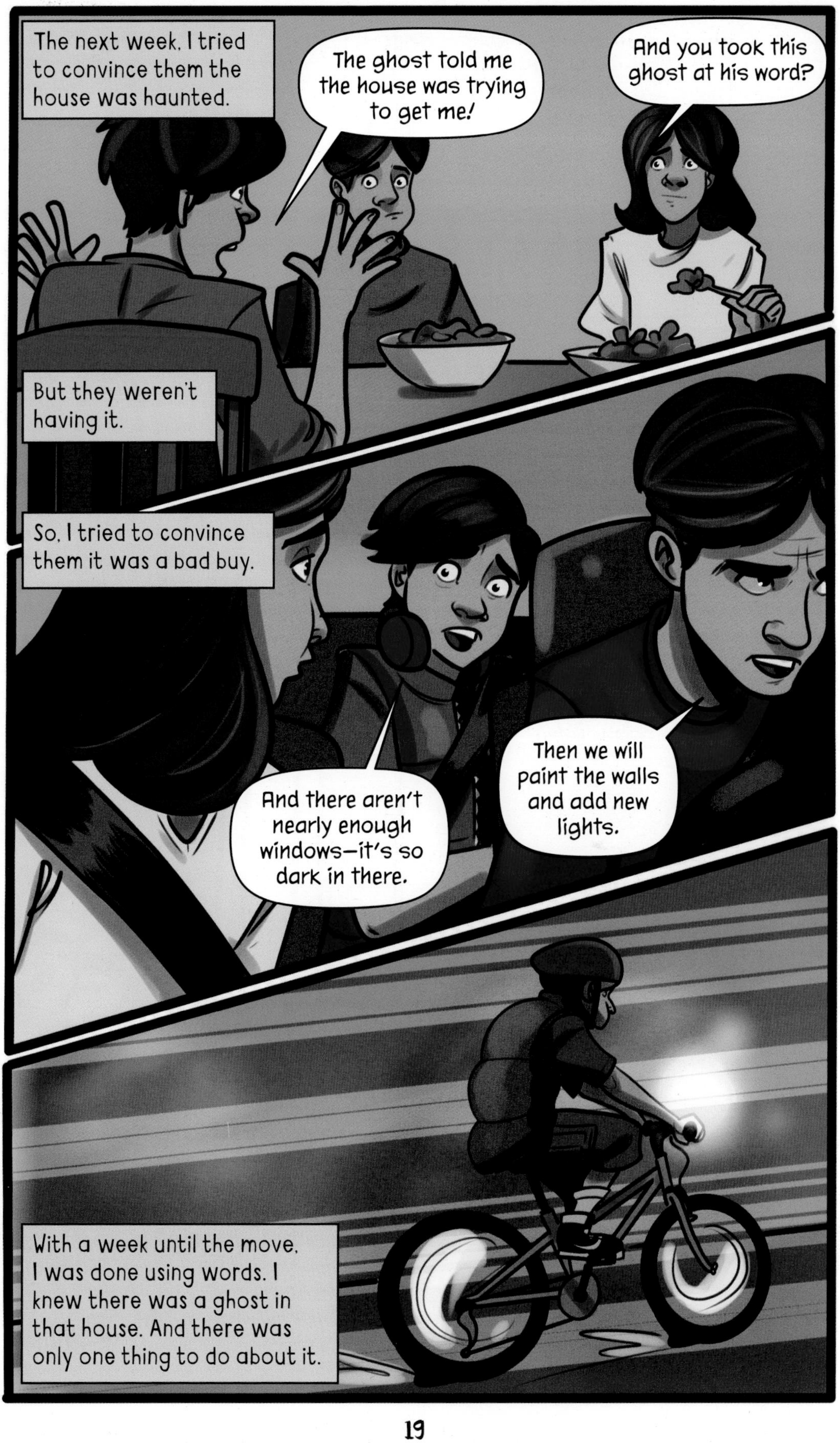

The next week, I tried to convince them the house was haunted.
The ghost told me the house was trying to get me!
And you took this ghost at his word?
But they weren't having it.
So, I tried to convince them it was a bad buy.
And there aren't nearly enough windows—it's so dark in there.
Then we will paint the walls and add new lights.
With a week until the move, I was done using words. I knew there was a ghost in that house. And there was only one thing to do about it.

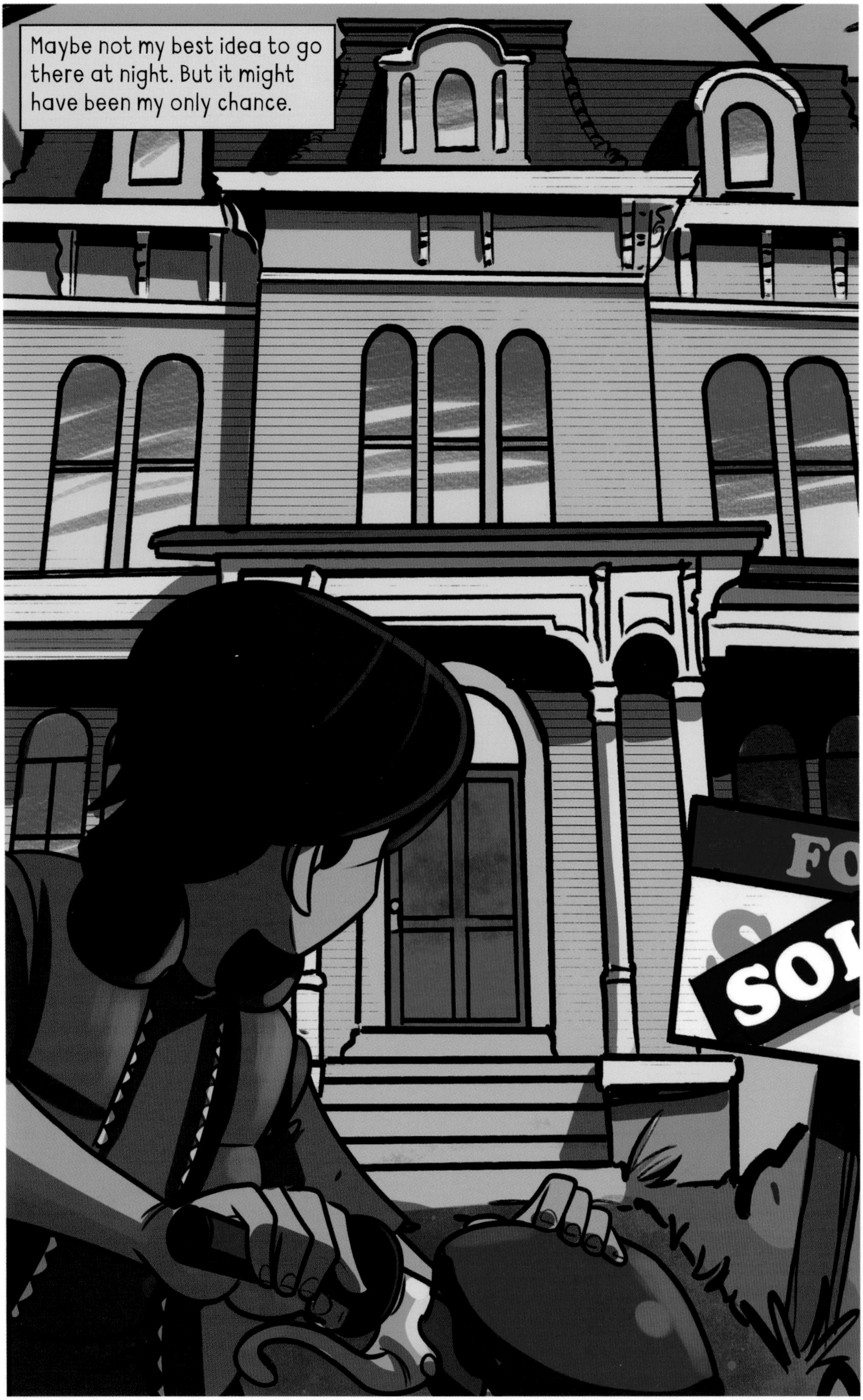
Maybe not my best idea to go there at night. But it might have been my only chance.
FO
SOL

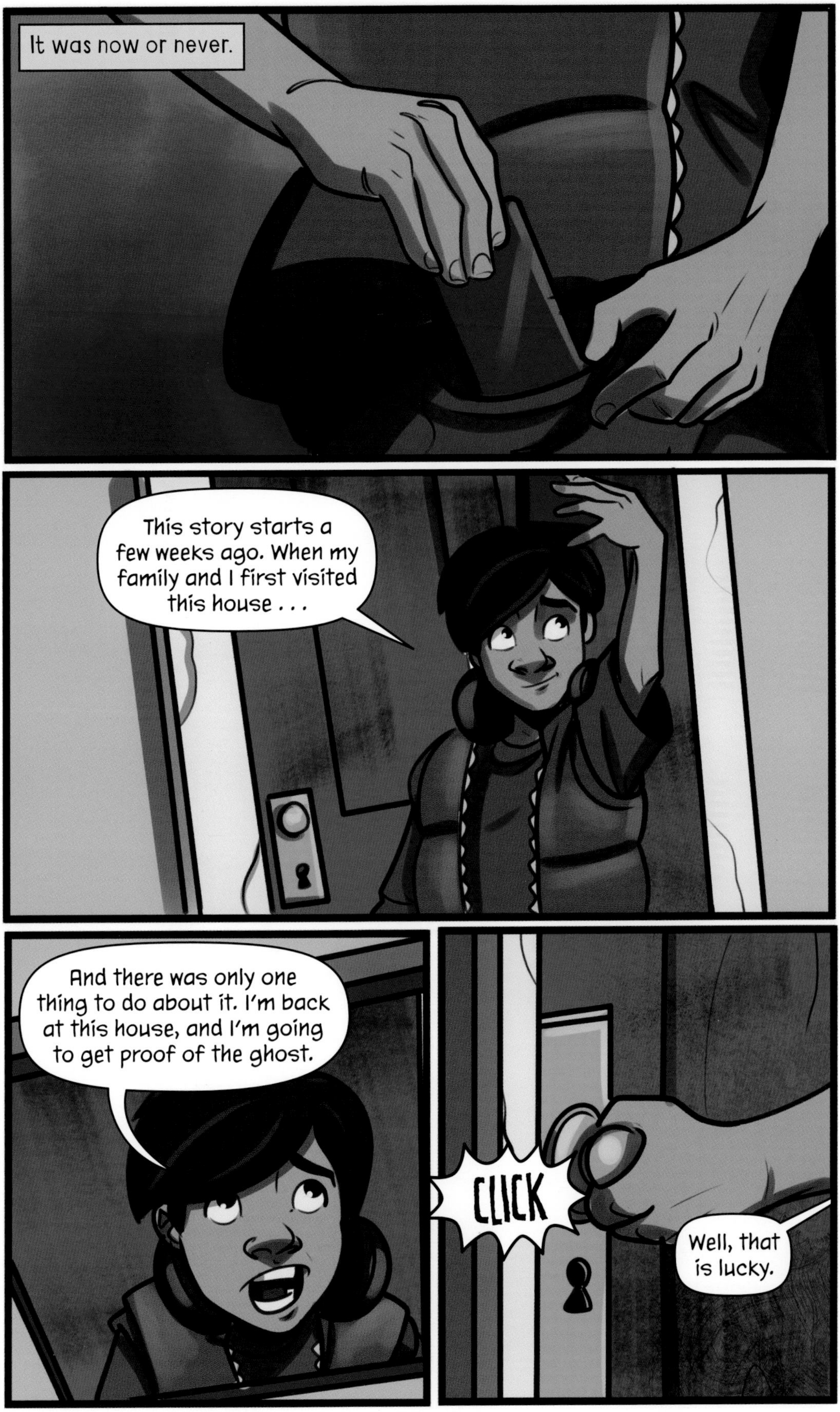
It was now or never.
This story starts a few weeks ago. When my family and I first visited this house . . .
And there was only one thing to do about it. I'm back at this house, and I'm going to get proof of the ghost.
CLICK
Well, that is lucky.

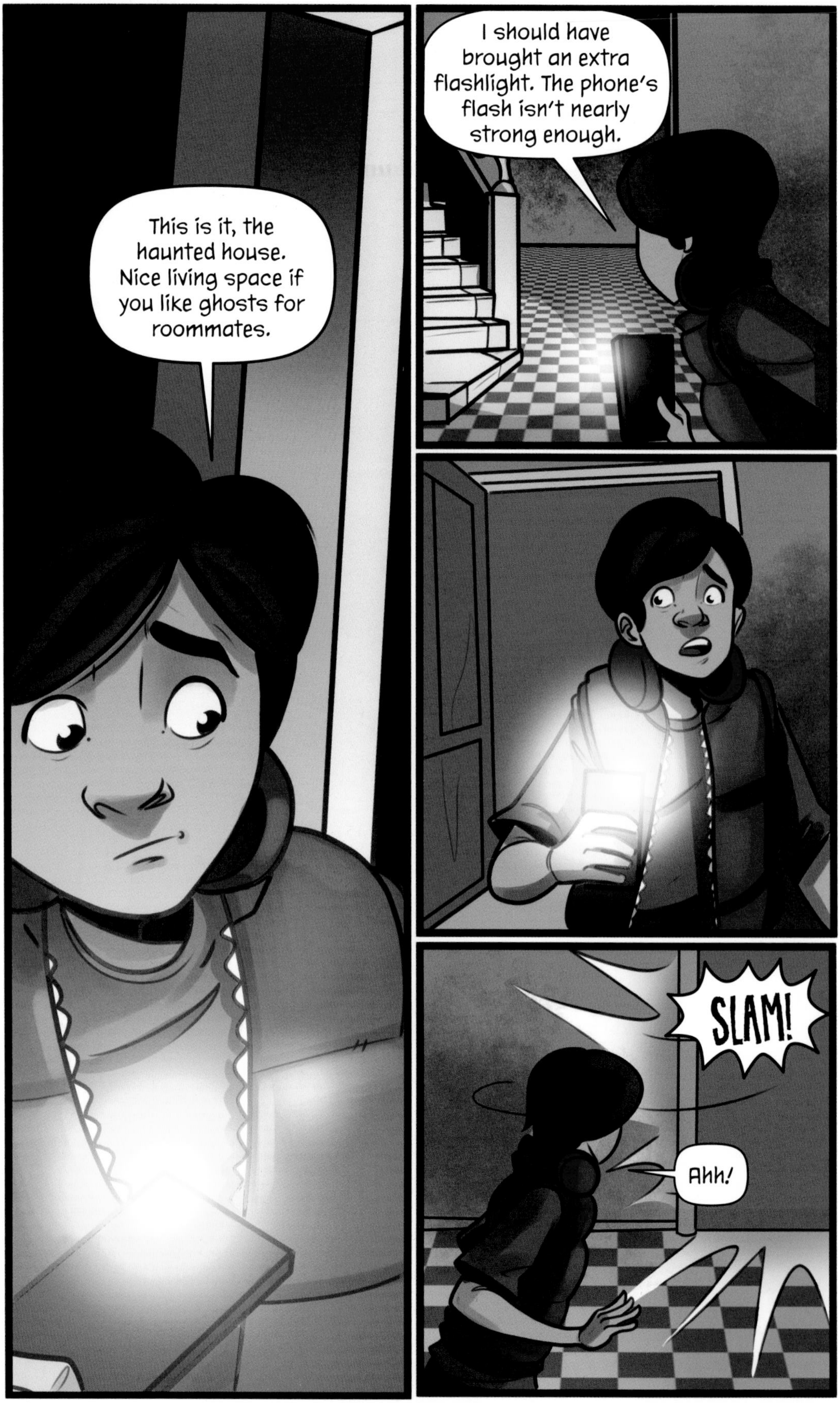
This is it, the haunted house. Nice living space if you like ghosts for roommates.
I should have brought an extra flashlight. The phone's flash isn't nearly strong enough.
SLAM!
Ahh!

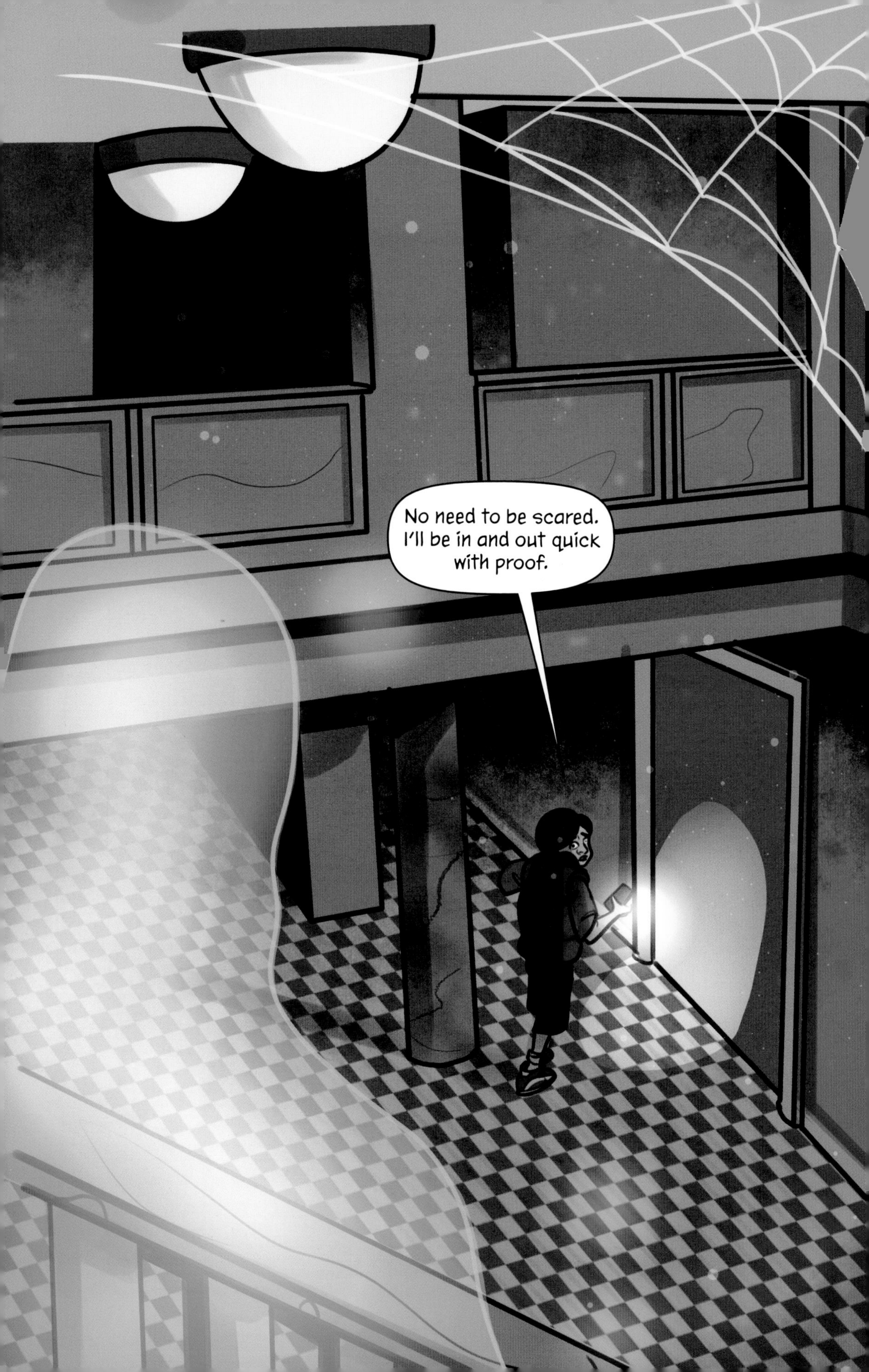
No need to be scared. I'll be in and out quick with proof.

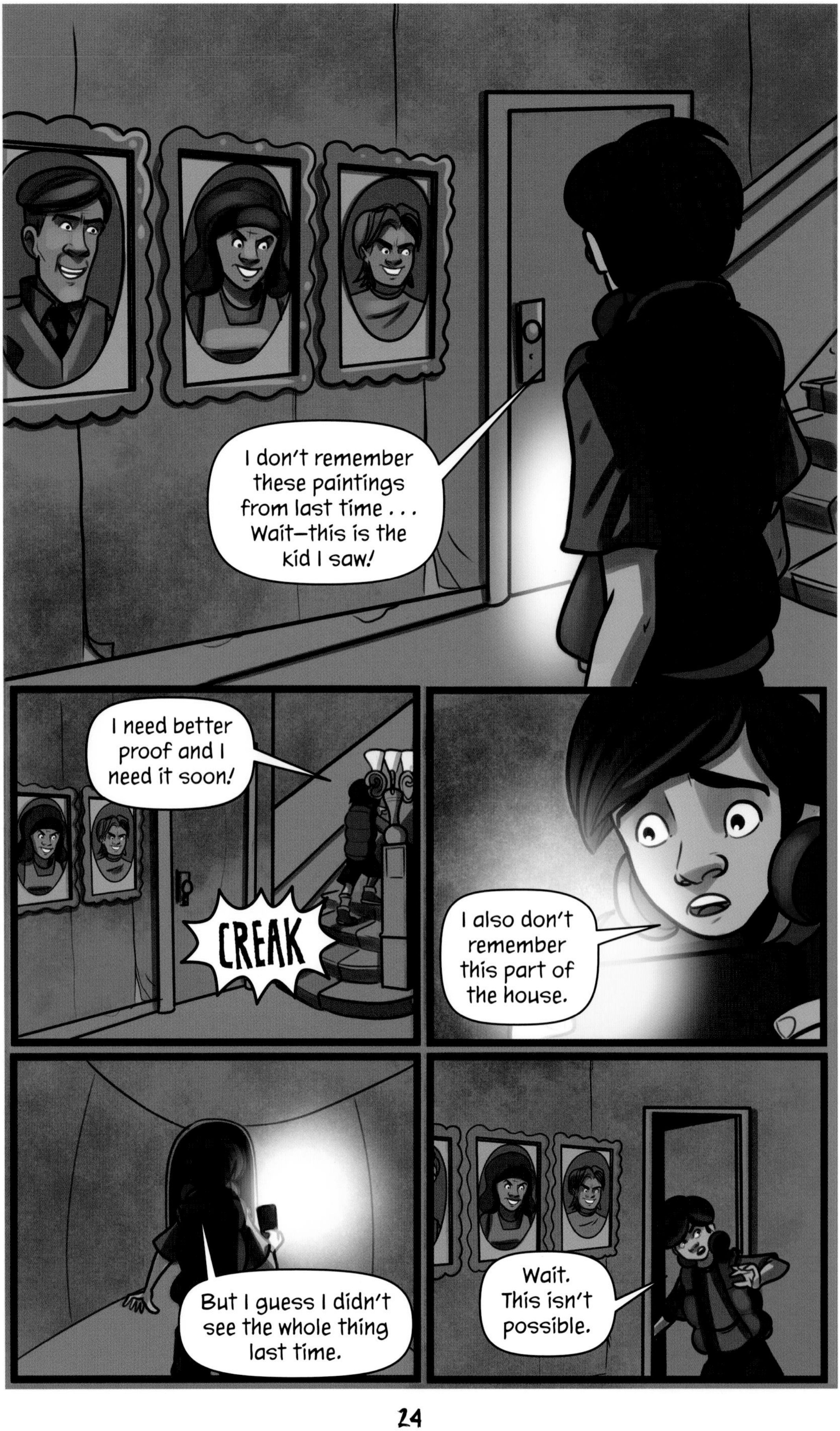
I don't remember these paintings from last time . . . Wait—this is the kid I saw!
I need better proof and I need it soon!
CREAK
I also don't remember this part of the house.
But I guess I didn't see the whole thing last time.
Wait. This isn't possible.

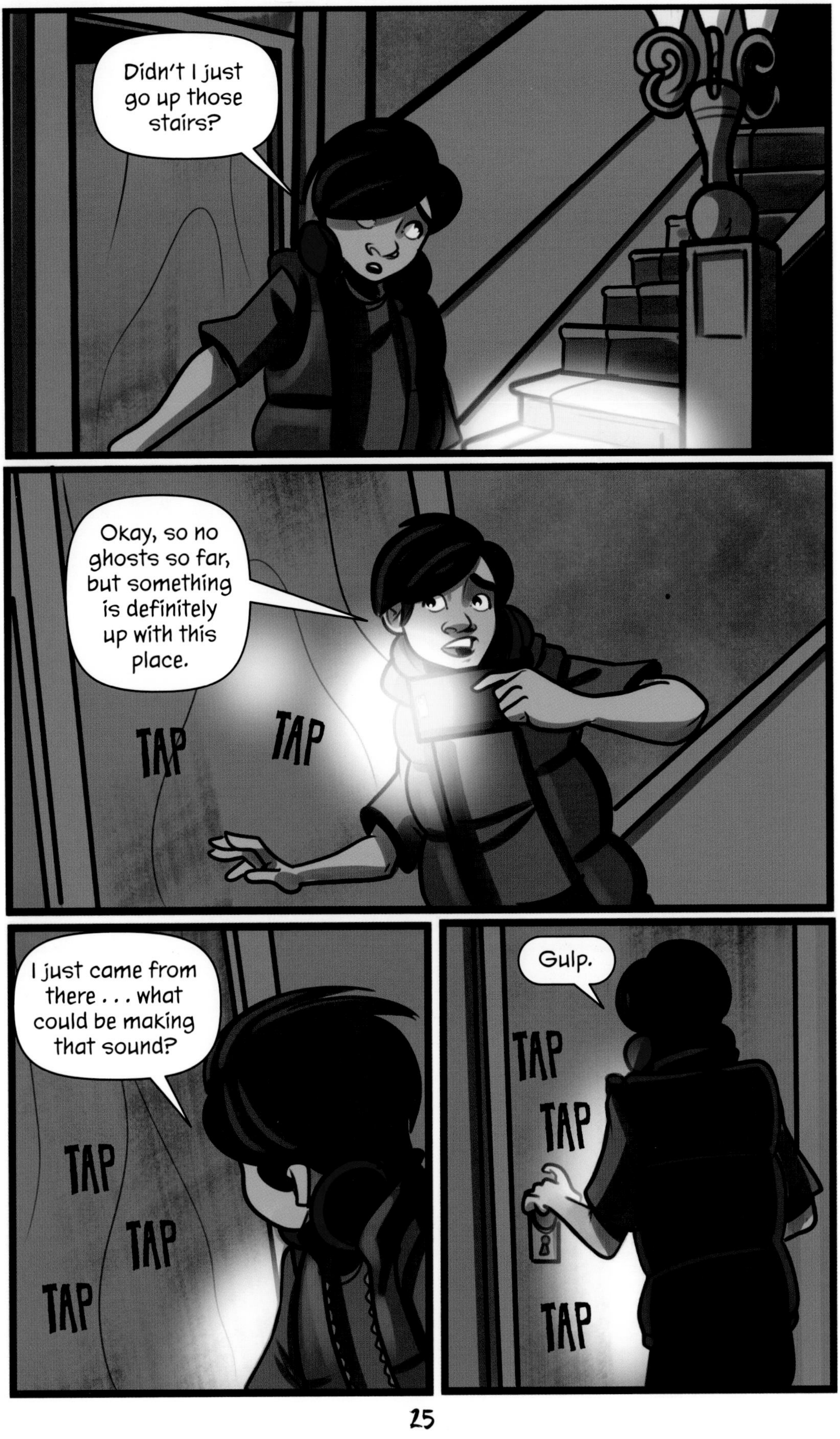
Didn't I just go up those stairs?
Okay, so no ghosts so far, but something is definitely up with this place.
TAP
TAP
I just came from there . . . what could be making that sound?
TAP
TAP
TAP
Gulp.
TAP
TAP
TAP

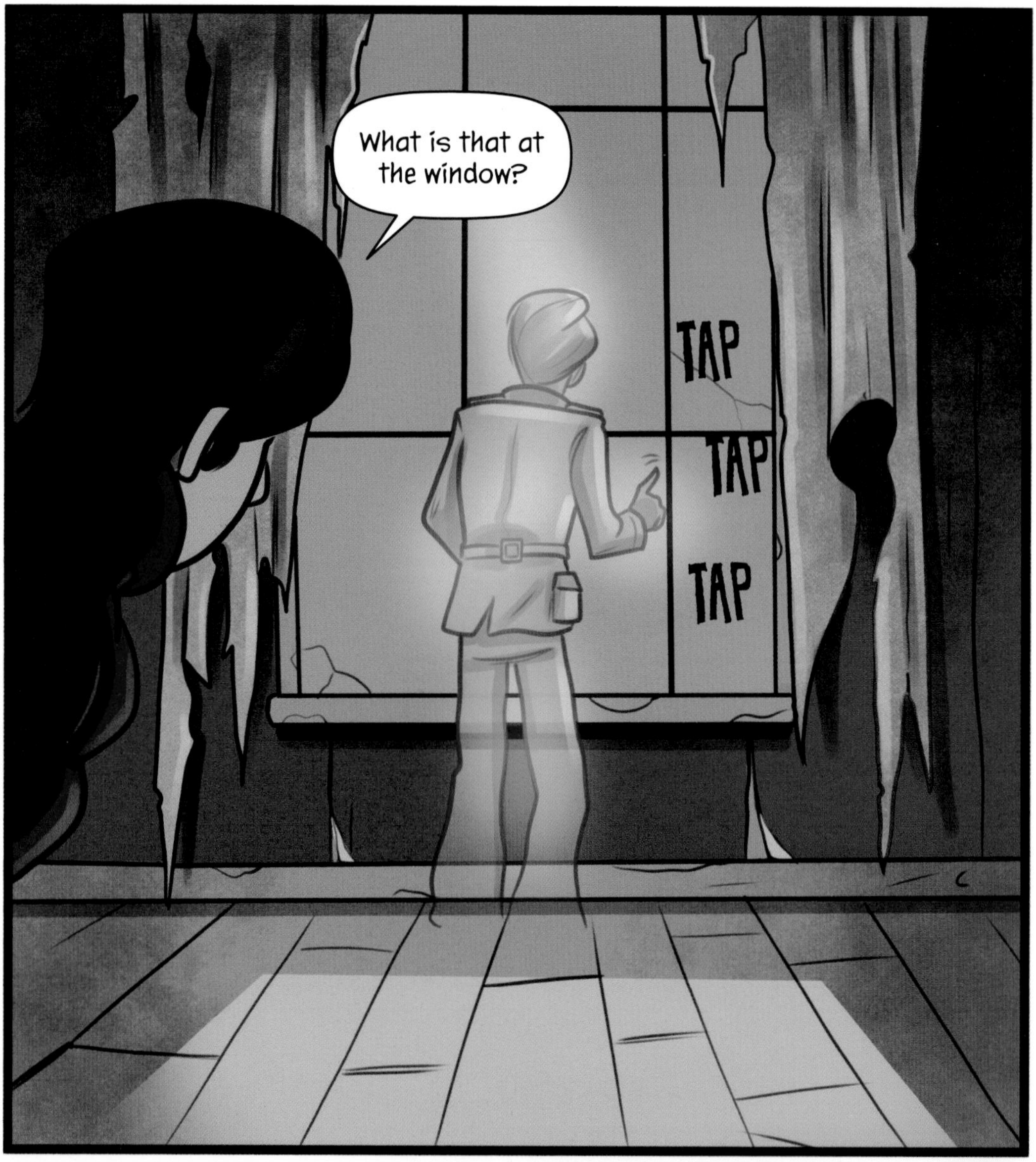
What is that at the window?
TAP
TAP
TAP

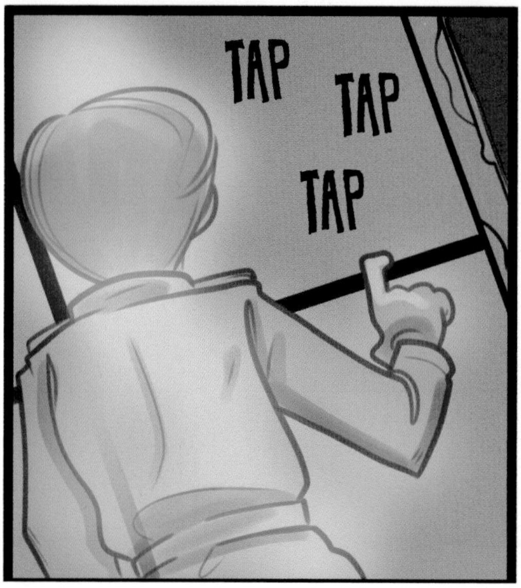
TAP
TAP
TAP

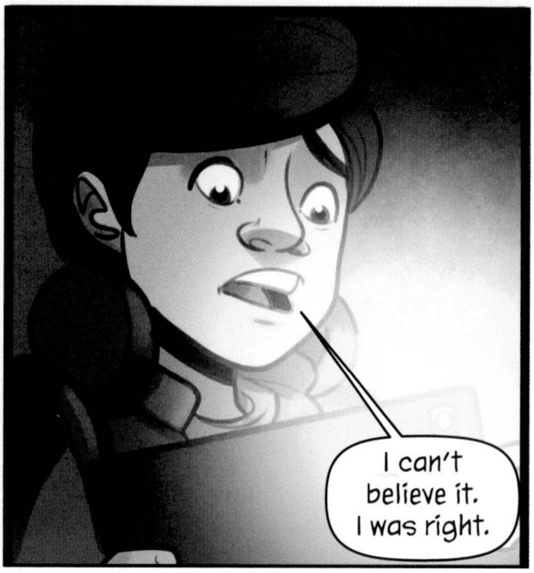
I can't believe it. I was right.

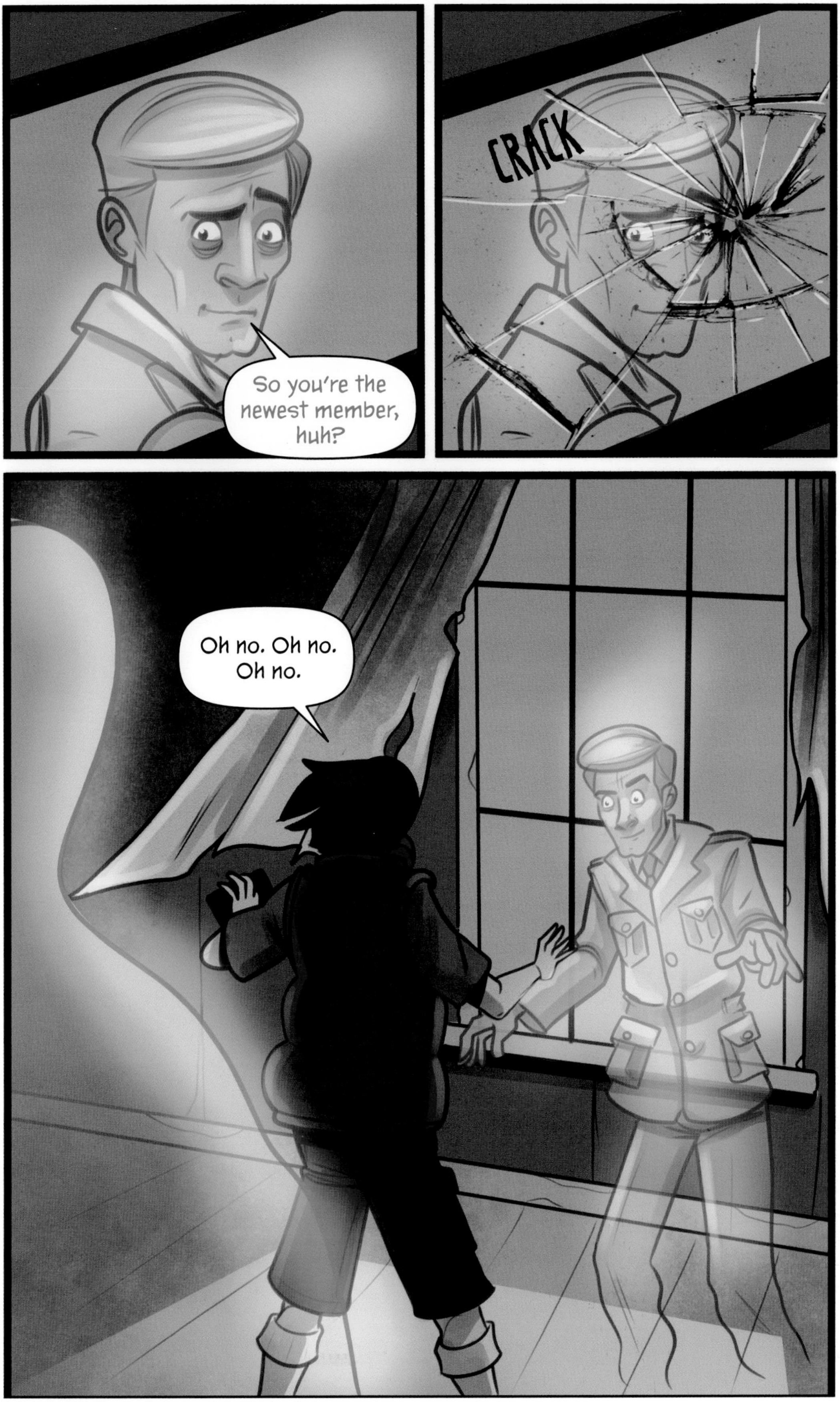
So you're the newest member, huh?
CRACK
Oh no. Oh no. Oh no.

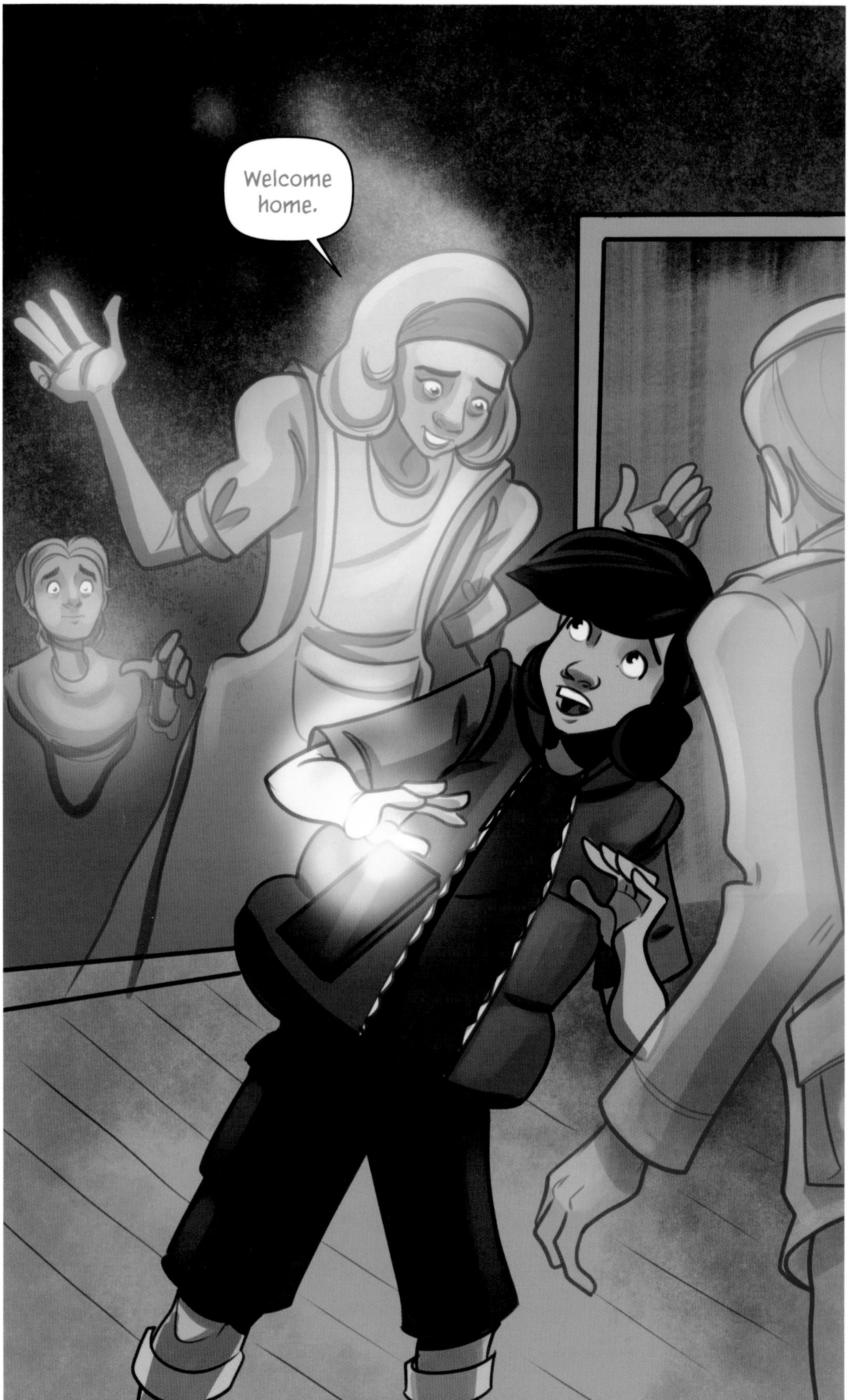
Welcome home.

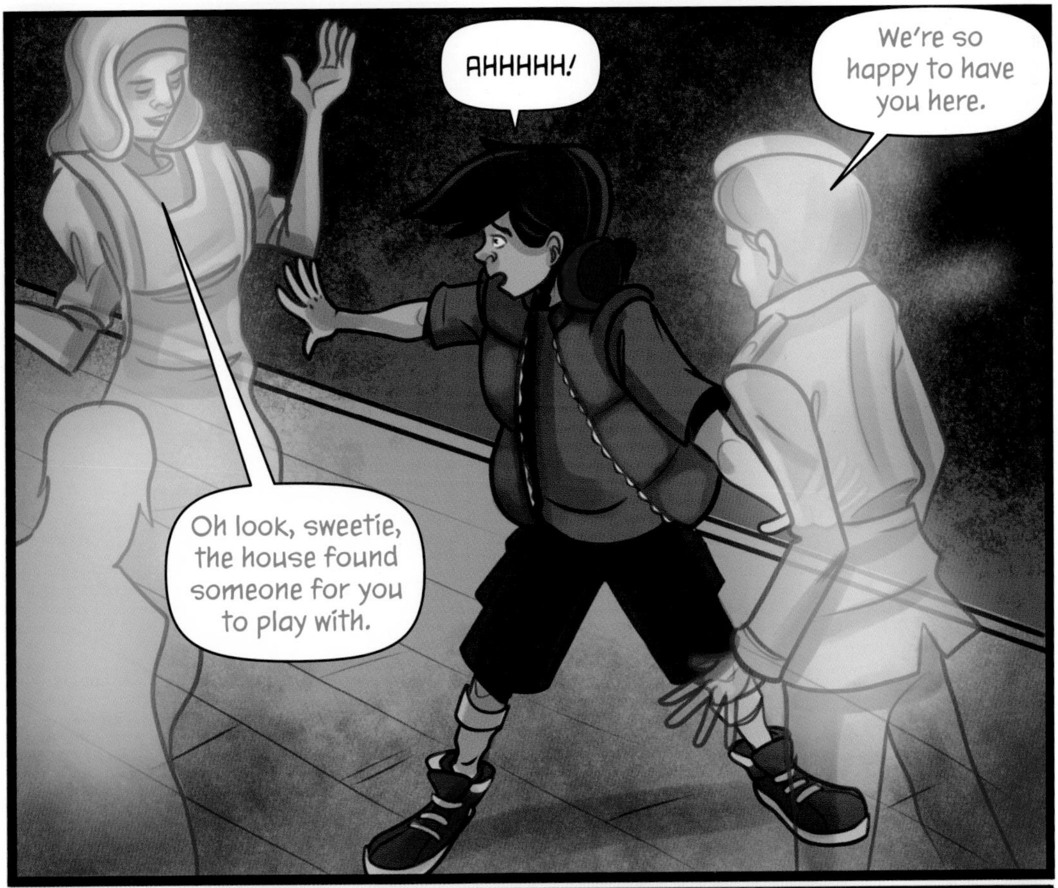
AHHHHH!
We're so happy to have you here.
Oh look, sweetie, the house found someone for you to play with.

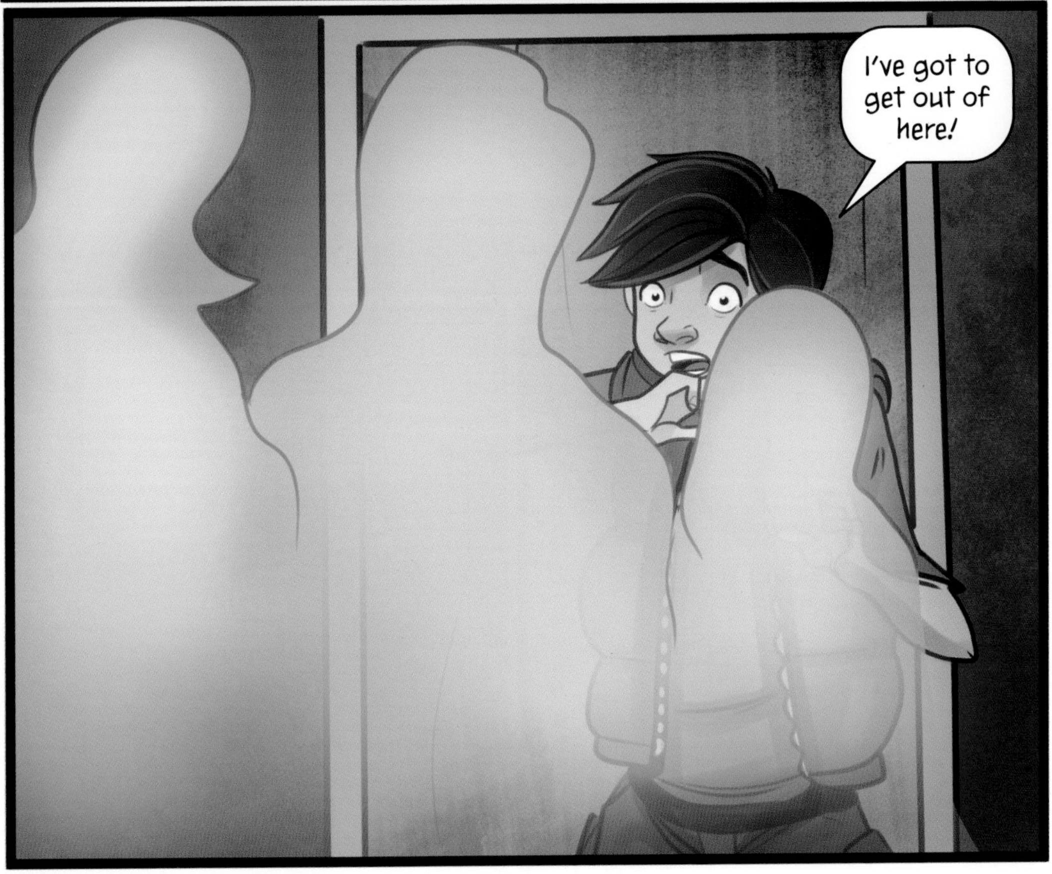
I've got to get out of here!

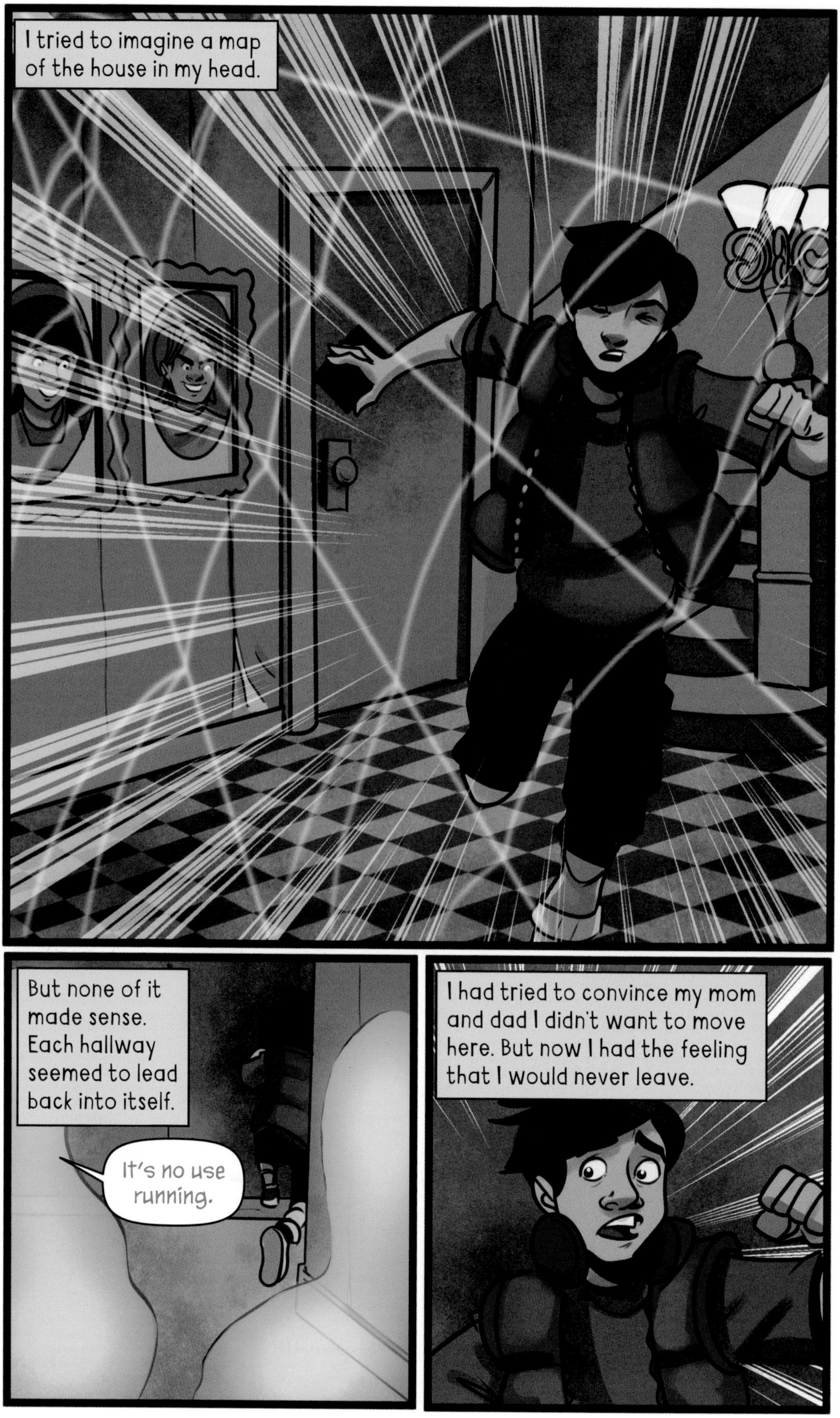
I tried to imagine a map of the house in my head.
But none of it made sense. Each hallway seemed to lead back into itself.
It's no use running.
I had tried to convince my mom and dad I didn't want to move here. But now I had the feeling that I would never leave.

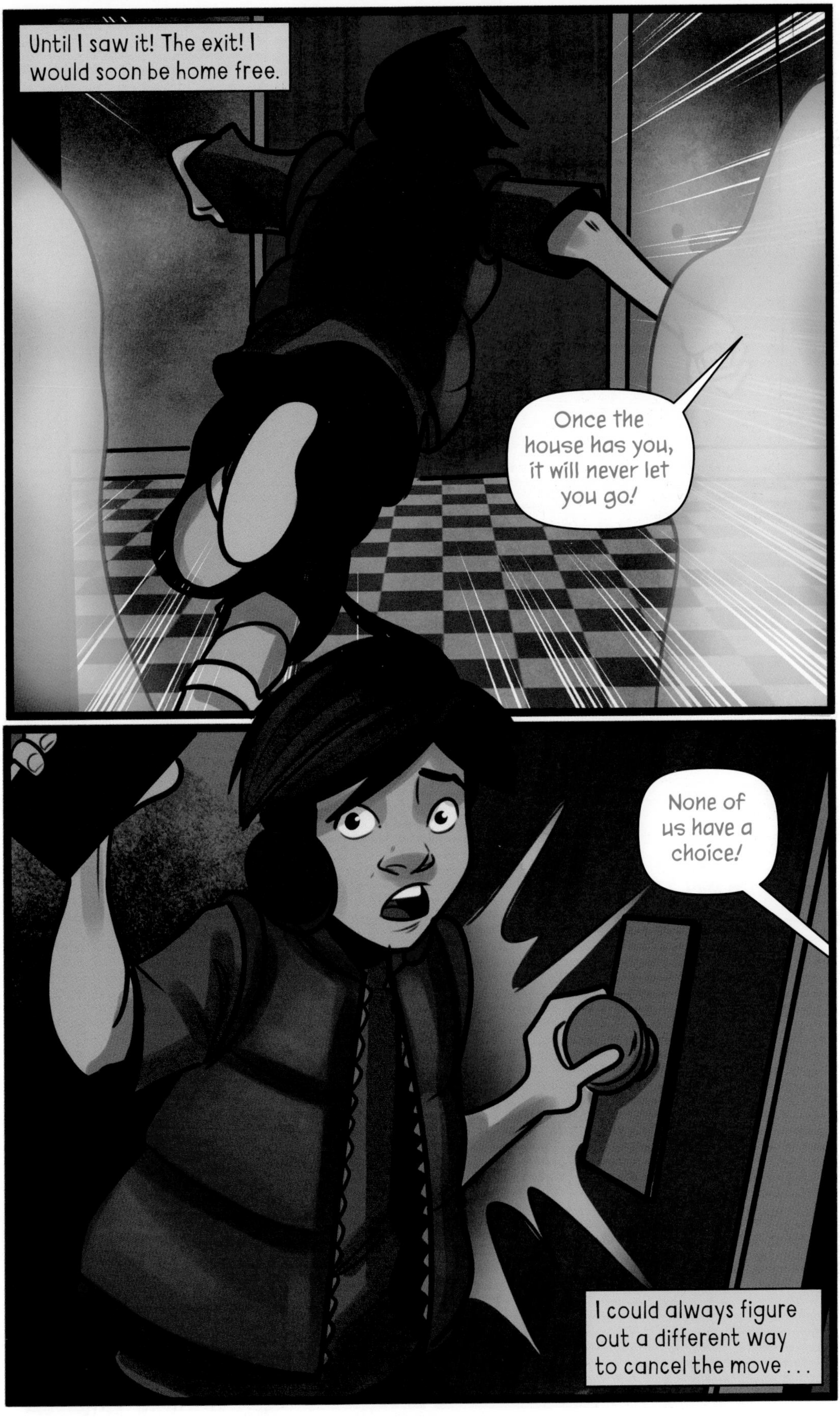
Until I saw it! The exit! I would soon be home free.
Once the house has you, it will never let you go!
None of us have a choice!
I could always figure out a different way to cancel the move . . .

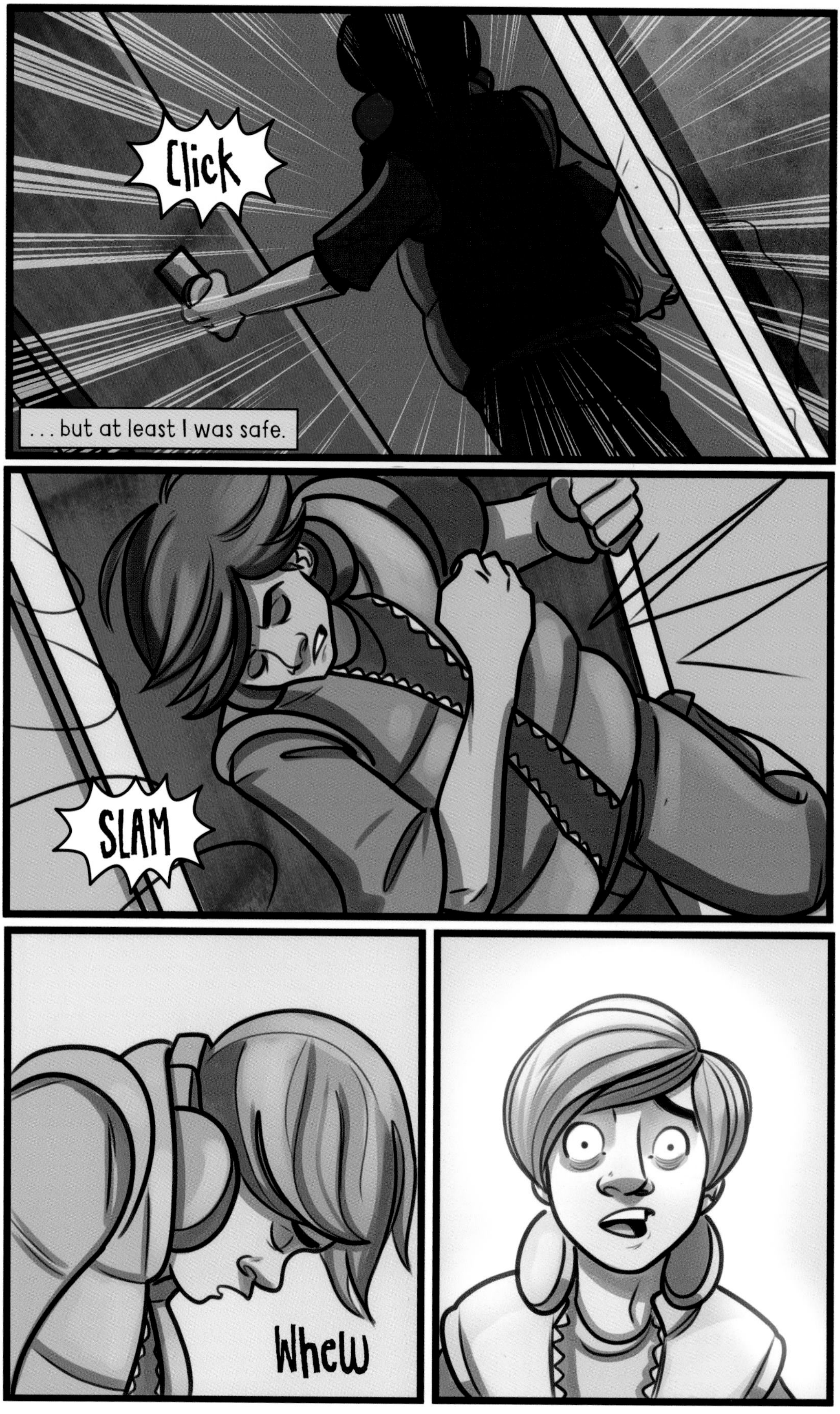
Click
. . . but at least I was safe.
SLAM
Whew

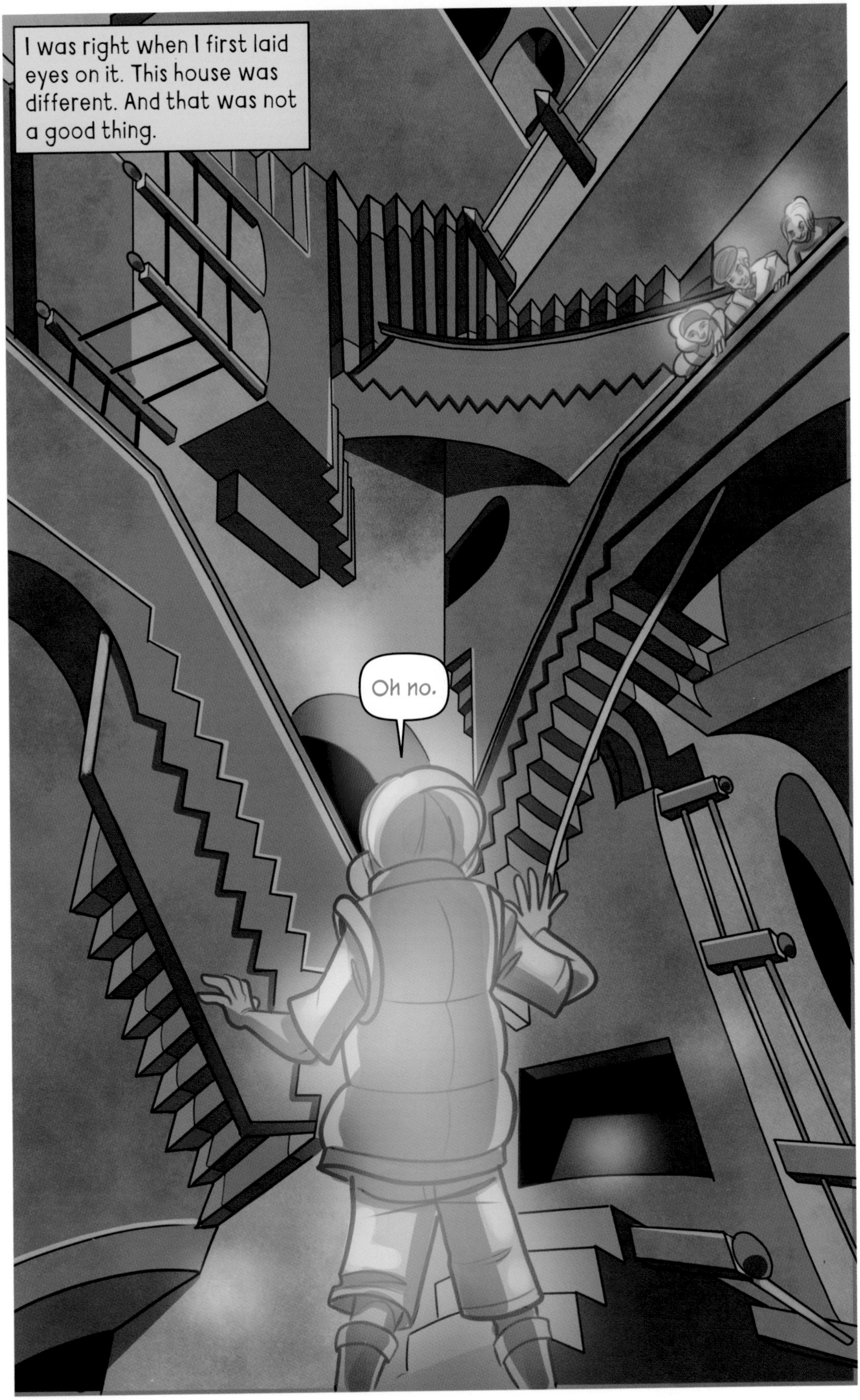
I was right when I first laid eyes on it. This house was different. And that was not a good thing.
Oh no.

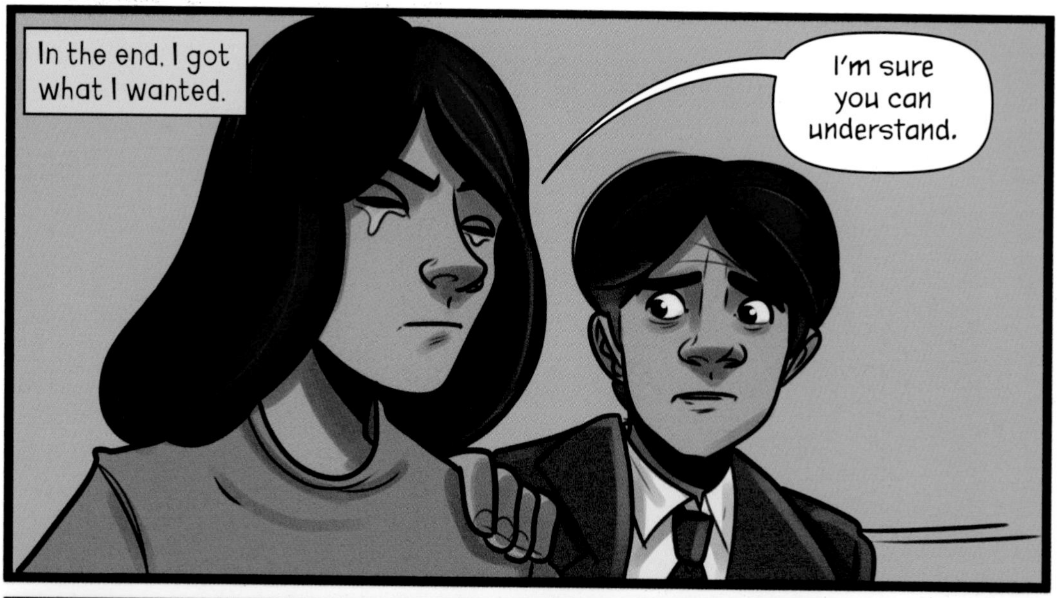
In the end, I got what I wanted.
I'm sure you can understand.

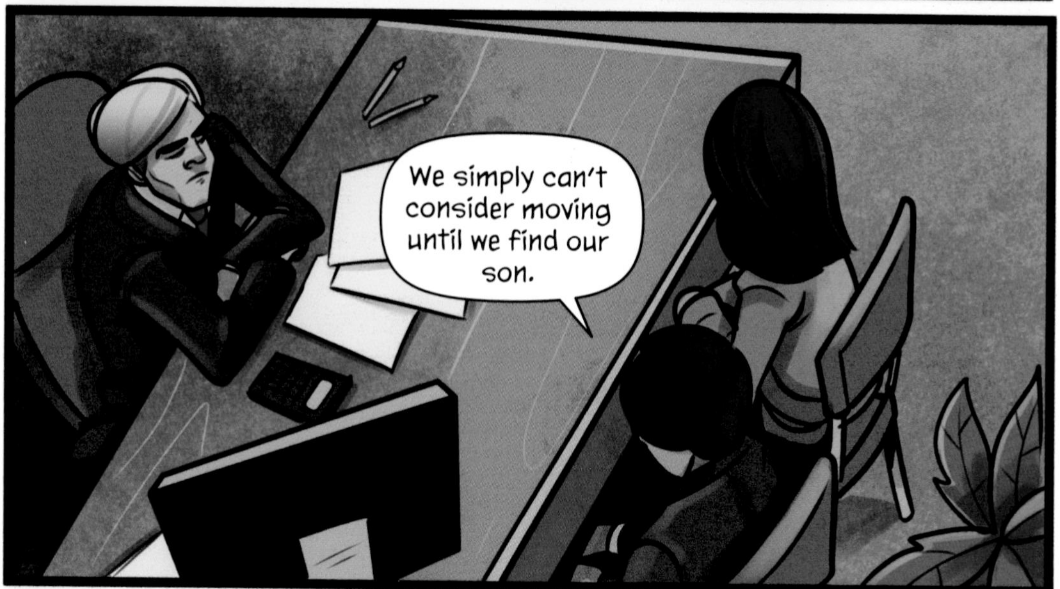
We simply can't consider moving until we find our son.

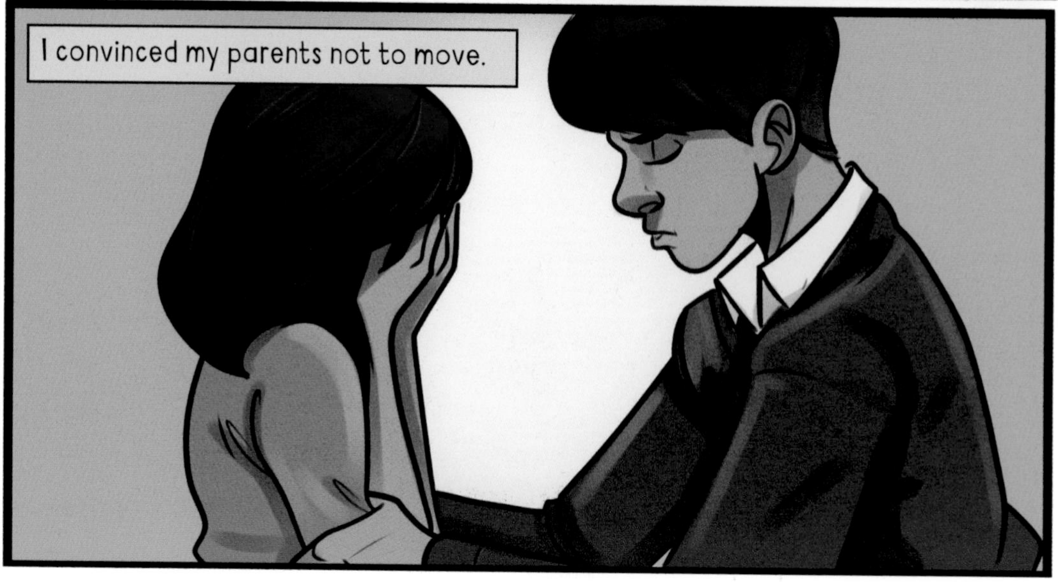
I convinced my parents not to move.

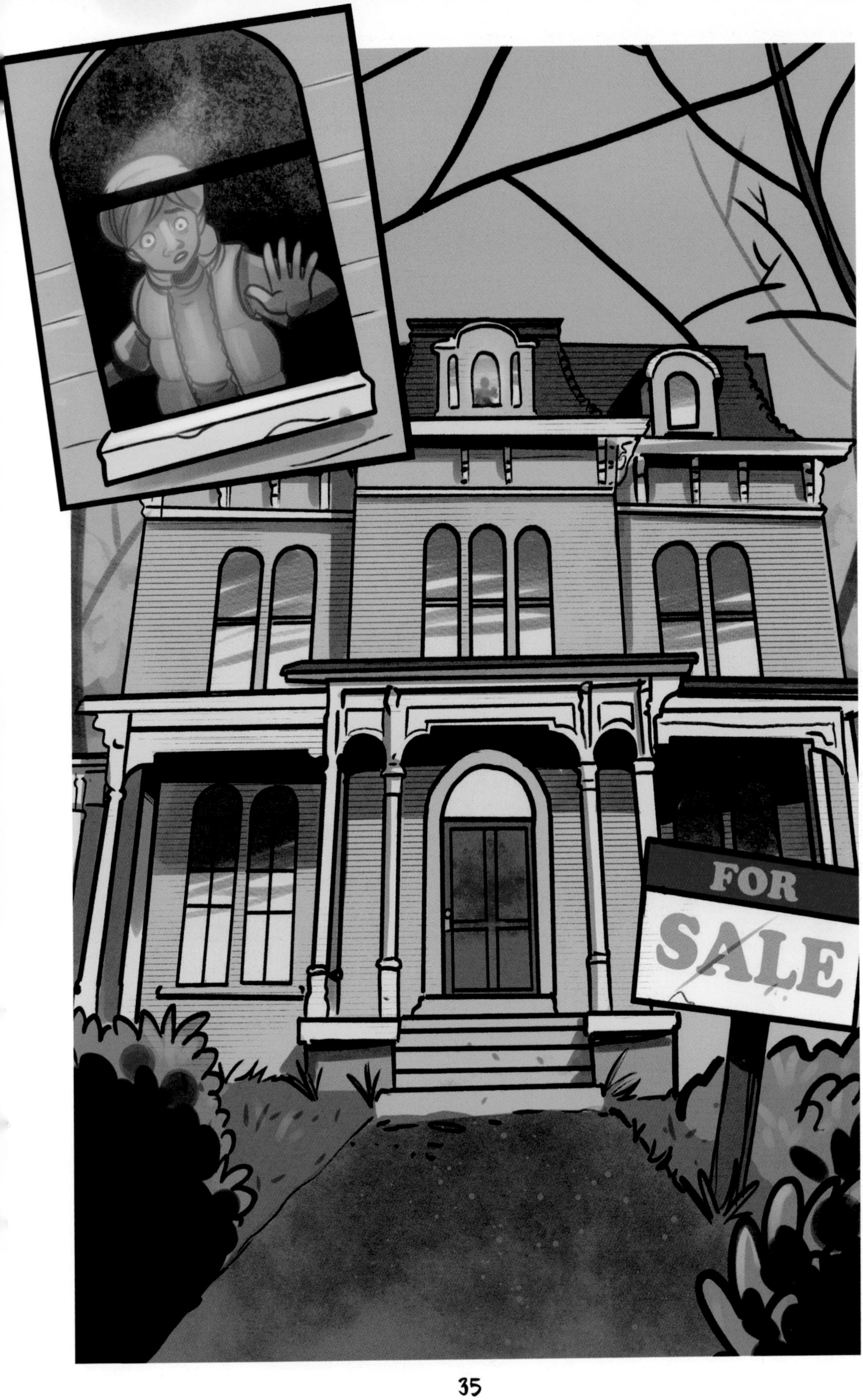
FOR
SALE

LOOK CLOSER

1. Who is making the TAP sounds here? Turn to pages 25 and 26 if you need help.

I just came from there . . . what could be making that sound?
TAP
TAP
TAP
TAP
TAP
TAP

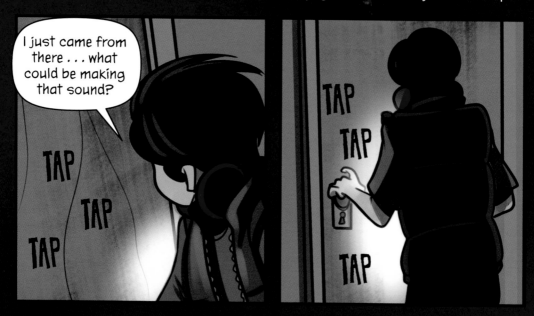

2. What has happened in these panels on page 27? How do you know?

So you're the newest member, huh?
CRACK

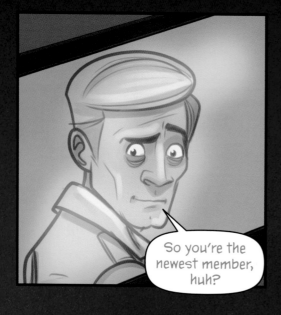

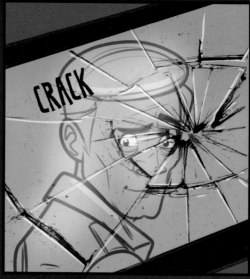

3. The illustrator uses lines and webbing to create a sense of confusion in this panel. Brainstorm other ways the art could have been drawn to show confusion.

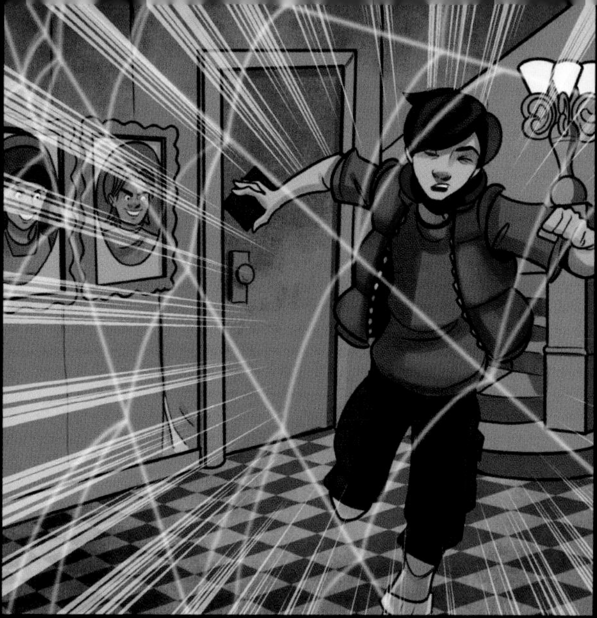

4. What has happened to Dominic by the end of the story? What clues tell you this?

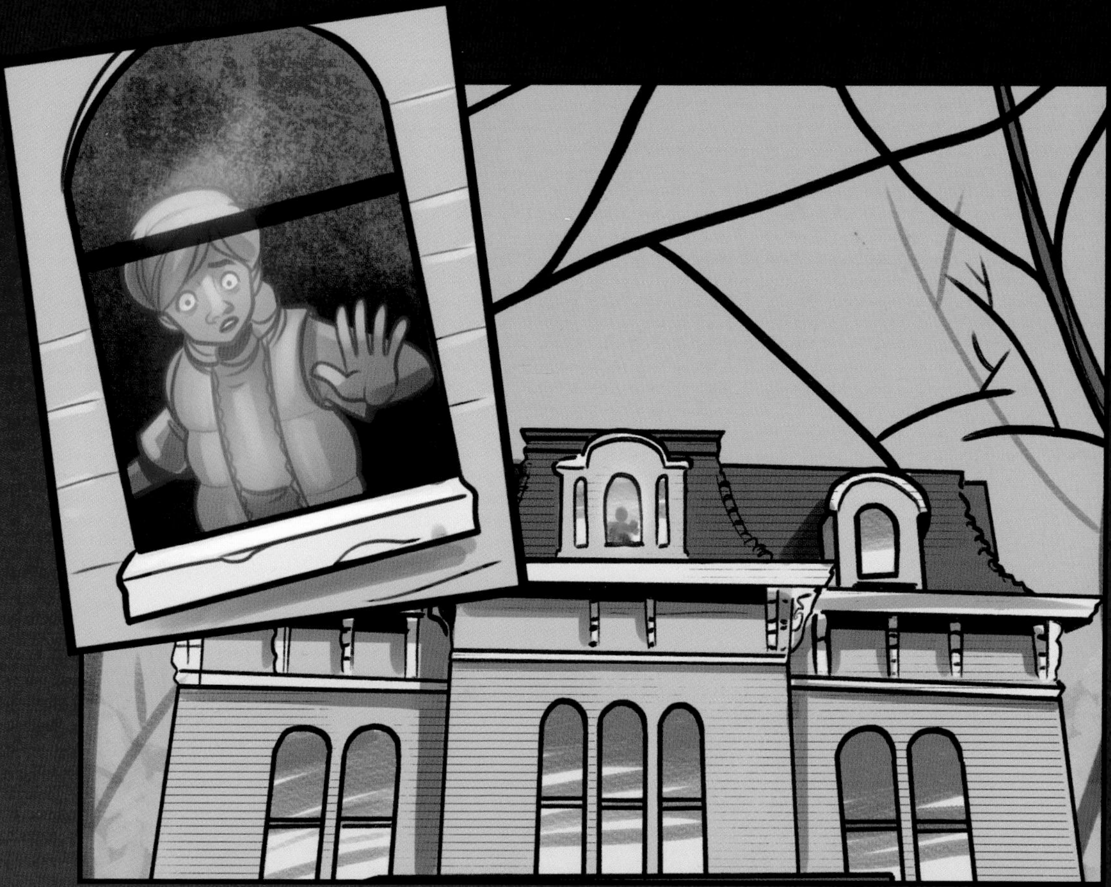

THE AUTHOR

Daniel Mauleón earned an MFA in Writing for Children and Young Adults at Hamline University in 2017. Since then, he has written fiction, nonfiction, and graphic novels for Capstone. He lives in Minneapolis, Minnesota, with his wife and two cats.

THE ILLUSTRATOR

Alan Brown is a freelance artist from the United Kingdom. He's worked on a variety of projects including Ben 10 Omniverse graphic novels for Viz Media, as well as children's book illustrations for the likes of HarperCollins and Watts. He has a keen interest in the comic book world, where he's at home creating bold graphic pieces. Alan works from an attic studio, along with his trusty sidekick, Ollie the miniature schnauzer, and his two sons, Wilf and Teddy.

GLOSSARY

architecture (AR-kuh-tek-chuhr)—the design of buildings

claim (KLAYM)—to take ownership or possession of

convince (kuhn-VINS)—to make a person believe or agree by arguing or showing proof

dud (DUHD)—a failure

house hunting (HOUS HUHN-ting)—to look for a house to rent or buy and live in

inappropriate (in-uh-PROH-pree-it)—not suitable or correct

prove (PROOV)—to show that something is true

realize (REE-uhl-ahyz)—to become aware of

Realtor (REE-uhl-tor)—a person who sells houses for a job

wander (WAHN-der)—to move about without a purpose

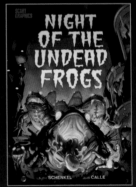